IN THE DIRECTION OF THE SUN

LUCY J. MADISON

Labrador Publishing

Editor: Nikki Busch

Labrador Publishing LLC

24 W. Main St. Suite 330

Clinton, CT 06413

www.labradorpublishing.com

Printed in the United States of America

Second Edition - March 5, 2018

*This book is affectionately dedicated to
my best friends Deb, Nella, Missy, and Carla.
We've been friends thirty years and counting
and not once have you ever gone hiking with me.
Just saying.*

"So bright the flames burned in our hearts
that we found each other in the dark."

- City and Colour

PART I

CHAPTER 1

ALEX

August 2014
Appalachian Trail at Sage's Ravine, Massachusetts

lex McKenzie wasn't at all the person she thought she was. She hadn't showered in over a week, and all she could think of was a cold beer, a hot shower, and a double cheeseburger—in that order. Alex shivered as she unrolled her sleeping bag on the wooden platform of the sparse, three-sided lean-to. The rain had been falling steadily on the Appalachian Trail near the Connecticut-Massachusetts border, making for an uncomfortable mid-August evening. Sleeping on a thin air mattress in the middle of the woods alone was miraculously never on her bucket list. Yet, here she was, a thirty-three-year-old woman taking her first official leap of faith.

Alex zipped up her sleeping bag, trying to rid her tall, slender body of the chill from being wet for hours on an unseasonably cool August day. She wrapped her shoulder-length dark hair in a bandana since it was still pretty damp and she could never sleep with wet hair plastered against the back of her neck. She went through her nighttime checklist: Toilet paper was positioned on her platform for easy reach in case she had to go during the night. Her pack hung from a hook a few feet off the ground on the other end of her sleeping platform to keep the mice away. So did her boots. Somewhere in New Hampshire, she'd learned that mice loved the salt from her dried sweat and would happily chew through bootlaces if given the opportunity. Her food and few toiletries hung safely from a tree about 150 feet away from the shelter in an Ursak bag specially designed to keep bear, mice, and anything else out.

She slid down inside the dry sleeping bag and was once again thankful she'd splurged on the Big Agnes Double Z Air Pad that was about a pound heavier than most other inflatable sleeping pads. When you carried everything on your back to survive, a pound was a lot of weight. But the added two inches of cushion and insulation was manna from the gods after a long and wet day hiking. Her stomach growled, a common occurrence after burning off over 5,000 calories and eating only beef jerky, ramen noodles, and a Snickers bar for dinner. The rain poured down outside creating a comforting wall of sound Alex had grown to love when she was snug inside a dry shelter for the night.

She reminded herself of the date, as she did each and every night before she fell asleep. It was August 13, 2014. She had no idea what day of the week it was, but she knew she had been hiking for seventy-five days.

The beam from her headlamp illuminated various initials and carvings on the wooden wall of the Sage's Ravine lean-to, which stood in a large gully surrounded by lush green and rocks. One could easily walk right by the shelter from above and never even know it was there at all. One phrase inside the darkened lean-to that was most likely carved by a previous hiker with a pocket knife caught her eye: "Only Love" it read. She stopped for a moment to soak in those two words. She was exhausted, but she wasn't too exhausted from a slippery and dangerous nine-mile hike in driving rain with a thirty-pound bag strapped to her back to ignore the inner workings of her mind. She repositioned her head on her lumpy, dry bag of dirty and smelly clothes and could do nothing but laugh at the irony of those words. Maybe it was just a coincidence or perhaps it was the universe sending her a sign. Either way, it bugged her. She clicked off her headlamp and hung it from a nail on the sidewall of the shelter for easy access. Those two words swirled around her mind like red wine in a crystal glass.

Most people labeled themselves by who they were to other people. Alex was a daughter, a sister, a teacher, a friend, and a lover. Her two best friends, Marcie and Emma, had known her since she was six years old. They knew all of her secrets and all of her hopes and dreams. Of course, both tried to talk Alex out of what she was about to do, but both also admitted they knew that once Alex set her mind to something, she would do it.

"You are so damned stubborn it's astonishing," said Marcie one evening when she came by to help Alex pack.

"I know I am," Alex said. "This is just something I feel I have to do. I can't explain it."

"Well you know Emma and I are here for you. We'll help your sister keep an eye on the house but we talked, and neither one of us is remotely interested in hiking with you."

Alex laughed. She loved her friends for their honesty and knew that if she needed them, they'd hike to the end of the earth for her. Her friends always had her back, and she had theirs.

That last part of being a lover—that one was tricky. Yes. She knew love, deep and true, albeit one-sided. No matter how hard she tried, she could not get that love out of her head. And apparently, chewing through miles on craggy trails wouldn't erase it. She knew that after hiking exactly 681.8 miles through Maine, New Hampshire, Vermont, and now Massachusetts over seventy-five days. Try as she might, she just couldn't make the pain in her heart fade away. She thought she could. She imagined that hiking the Appalachian Trail would be this magical, mystical ride where she could pack up her past heartbreak and leave it all behind her as the miles stretched out like a big yawn in front of her. Books like *A Walk in The Woods* and *Wild* only fueled her misshapen belief that hiking any trail, let alone the famed Appalachian Trail, would be this spiritual healing journey. She recalled the wisdom her grandfather told her one afternoon when he had taken her out for an ice cream cone. She was about fourteen years old. He said in his inimitable Yogi Berra way, "It doesn't matter where you go. You take you with you no matter what." She never fully understood the meaning of those words until now. She carried that past with her—every step, every mile, every stream crossed, and every rainy day. Her past was added weight, and her wounded heart beat all the same, no matter where she found herself laying her head for the night.

The only bonus she found was being so tired after hiking all day that she rarely remained awake more than ten minutes before she was sacked out in a near coma for the remainder of the night. On the flip side, it meant she now had the entire day of hiking in solitude to turn every memory and daydream over and over in her mind like a piece of sea glass in her hands.

Most already slightly insane Appalachian Trail hikers began their journeys at Springer Mountain, Georgia in February or March where the weather was warmer so they could hopefully end their epic 2,180-mile journeys in Maine at the summit of Mount Katahdin in September. She was the exception to the rule, as usual.

Alex chose a southbound route, starting May 30, 2014, specifically to avoid as many people as possible. She didn't want company. In 2013, only a mere 336 people reported completing a southbound thru-hike to the Appalachian Trail Conservancy from Mount Katahdin in Maine to Springer Mountain in Georgia. She knew the odds were stacked against her from the beginning and she was well aware of the extreme physical challenge she was throwing herself headlong into, alone, to start the hike. Her only goal was to get away from her life as fast as possible and, oddly enough, this was the only way that made sense to her.

Alex thought about her first three weeks on the Appalachian Trail. She climbed Mount Katahdin, the highest and most challenging mountain on the entire Trail. Just the memory of her burning legs and muscle soreness made her cringe. She survived the one-hundred-mile wilderness in Maine with the black fly season in full swing. One night the flies were so bad she screamed at them for three hours until her voice went hoarse. Hypothermia was a real threat on more than one occasion when she fell into icy streams during several crossings. Even with all of the physical and mental challenges of the first few months, she survived Maine, New Hampshire, Vermont, and Massachusetts and learned to thrive through arguably the most difficult section of the Trail. She'd wanted to make things as challenging as possible from the beginning to get her mind off her heartbreak. That was her one motivating reason for attempting a solo southbound thru-hike. So far, however, it wasn't working. Her mind still found a way to work overtime despite the physical challenges.

When Alex told her mother and sister that she wanted to hike the Appalachian Trail alone, they thought she'd completely lost her mind. "Why on earth would you do that?" her mother asked, eyes wide, mouth hanging open in disbelief. For weeks Alex worked to convince them that not only did she have a plan, she had also been researching and testing gear for months (a slight white lie). Alex showed them detailed maps and route plans, her organized mail drop system to ensure supplies were readily available. She even went on a solo shakedown hike to make sure the gear she carried was the gear she actually needed since most thru-hikers end up ditching a third of their packs in the first two weeks anyway. She learned quickly that only those items she could not live without were worth carrying every step of the way. When she set her mind to something, there was no stopping her. She made the decision to hike the whole of the Appalachian Trail, and she would do it, no matter how difficult the journey ahead. Stubborn. She had been told she was stubborn more times than she could count.

Alex knew her mother only wanted the best for her, but she also knew full well that her mother didn't really know her. Her dear mother, Sally McKenzie, believed her daughter was a single woman in her early thirties with a respectable job as an English teacher in Stockbridge, a small, quaint, Massachusetts town. Alex never doubted her mother's fierce love but she also never felt as though her mother saw the real her. Of all her mother's skills, one of her worst flaws was only seeing what she wanted to see when she wanted to see it. She ignored anything that fell outside that rule. Like the part about Alex being a lesbian. She was on a constant merry-go-round of denial when it came to that subject even though Alex had told her years ago. Her mother never mentioned it again and pretended as though she'd never heard it. Not that Alex cared. She was past the point in her life when she needed her mother's acceptance. She was content with who she was, and she had come to terms long ago with the understanding that her mother loved her but would never know the real her.

Her sister Sara, on the other hand, knew Alex like the back of her own hand. One thing Alex loved about her older sister was how fiercely protective she was. It had always been just the two of them—Alex and Sara—taking on the world together. They survived their beloved father's death in a training mission at Hanscom Air Force Base when Sara was twelve years old, and Alex was two years younger and held hands as the honor guard at Arlington National Cemetery fired blanks into the air at his military funeral. They survived their first heartbreaks, acne, algebra, and high school side by side. They even chose to attend Amherst College together and roomed together for two years, remaining best friends and inseparable every step of the way. Sure, they had their knock-down, drag-out fights, but they never went to bed angry at one another, and they always had each other's backs.

A few days before Sara dropped Alex off in Maine, she'd stopped by to help her pack and go over the details for mail drops and taking care of the house one more time. Four years ago, Alex had bought the small Cape on Interlaken-Lake Drive—a quaint, and quiet area that had great walkability and charm. The house needed work, but over the years Alex transformed it doing just about every DIY project imaginable, from renovating the kitchen and bathrooms to knocking down walls to open up the living space. After several years and a seemingly endless cycle of projects, Alex finally had the house she'd envisioned ever since bidding on the place. It was her home, and she was apprehensive about leaving it for such a long period. The house had become a part of her. Every wall, every nail, every hardwood plank was personal to her. Leaving it for such a prolonged period made her stomach bottom out, yet she had no choice but to ask her sister to help out in her absence.

Although Sara had her own career as a dental hygienist and a new husband (she and David had been dating since college), she promised to take care of Alex's house and check in on it every few days. Alex knew Sara was trying desperately to keep an open mind about her baby sister walking into the wilderness alone for six months, maybe more. But the look on Sara's face told Alex she was unsuccessful in that attempt.

"I just don't understand why you are doing this," Sara said as the two sat outside on the porch, their feet dangling from the swinging bench. "You're cutting out almost a month before the school year ends and using the last of your sick time. Not to mention the leave of absence you're taking until December."

"I know, Sara. I've considered all of this," Alex responded. Actually, Alex had thought of nothing else for the last two weeks. Her bouts of worry and sleeplessness rotated between leaving her precious students before the school year ended to take a leave of absence during the start of the next year.

Sara continued on as if she had prepared this speech and

would say it all no matter what. "That job was so difficult for you to land. What if they don't want you back afterward? Do you have to leave everyone behind and go off alone like this? I'm trying, Alex, but I just don't understand it. You're giving up all your stability to go for a long walk."

"Are you done?" asked Alex.

"Yes, I think so."

Alex was silent for a moment. She leaned up against her sister and took a deep breath before speaking. "We've always done things together, and it must be hard knowing you won't be there to look out for me. I can't explain it. It's something I have to do. I'm no good to my students. I'm all out of focus. I need to clear my head, and this is the only way I can think to do it. You know how much I've loved to hike ever since Daddy took us to Bear Mountain. Being in the woods does something to me. It clears my head and my soul. Please try to understand I'm not walking away from you or from Mom."

Sara raised an eyebrow at Alex.

"Okay, maybe I am walking away from Mom. Can you blame me?" Alex quickly added, "But not you. Never you. Please believe me, Sara. I need to take a leap. I need to live a little. I can't just stay here in Stockbridge and stagnate." Alex wrapped her arms around Sara's waist and leaned in, comforted by her sister's protectiveness.

"What if something happens to you?" Sara's voice cracked.

"You know I have the satellite communicator. You'll be able to track my location every ten minutes." Alex patted her leg, trying to make Sara believe she had thought of every detail. "I'm carrying extra battery chargers just to make sure I always have it powered up. And we can text with it even if I don't have cell service. Nothing is going to happen, or if it does, I can handle it."

"I just hate the idea of you being out there all alone."

"See, that's the part I am most thrilled about."

"Is this about her?"

"What do you mean?" asked Alex with feigned cluelessness.

Again, Sara arched an eyebrow at her younger sister.

"It might be. A little bit." Alex shrugged her shoulders. "Maybe more than a little bit."

"Oh, babe. If I could take away that heartbreak for you, I'd do it in a second." Sara hugged her tighter.

"I know," Alex sighed. "I wish you could too." She was silent for a time. It had only been a month since she'd last spoken to Cate. A long, hard month. "I just can't get past it," she finally admitted, her voice wavering. "Cate took something from me, and no matter how hard I try, I can't get it back. All the love I had to give wasn't enough for her." Alex roughly brushed away the tears that slid down her face. She would not cry, not in front of her sister.

Alex thought about her mother and her sister as the rain fell outside the shelter. Her stomach lurched at the twinges of homesickness she still felt whenever she thought about her sister or her little house. She wondered if Sara was watering the roses in the backyard enough. Her thoughts floated around on wafer-thin ribbons of emotion. Part of her nightly ritual included writing a letter to Cate in her mind. The words formed shapes in the darkness and gave meaning to her days even though she had carried a journal with the expectation of writing about her journey. Somehow writing her thoughts on paper seemed too final, too permanent, but her imaginary nightly letters to Cate formed then floated away into the darkness never to be repeated again. That was oddly comforting to her, and she continued her ritual, night after night for seventy-five days, speaking to Cate in her mind, holding tightly to that secret place in her own heart that no longer held solace.

Dear Cate: Today was a good day even though it rained. Whenever I walk in the rain, I am amazed at how quiet everything is around me. I can't hear my own boots hit the ground. Everything is muffled except for the raindrops hitting the summer leaves. As I walked today, I remembered the time you kissed me that night in your loft after you showed me all your art. You took me by surprise. You kept whispering, "This is for you." At first, I didn't know what you meant by that, but now I do. You said you never felt the way I did. Now, after I've been able to think about things, I realize you pitied me. You thought you were giving me a gift that day—a gift of the love I wanted so badly from you. But all you did was make things worse.

There was so much she wanted to say to Cate, but after their last conversation, it was as if everything froze except Alex. Her heart froze. Her mind froze. Nothing else mattered as days went flying by. Again, her mind returned to the words carved into the wood not three feet from her head. "Only Love." But love wasn't enough. Not this time.

Alex tried to sleep and couldn't. She put on her headlamp and scooted like an inchworm in her sleeping bag across the worn wooden plank platform until she could reach her backpack hanging on a hook. She rummaged around and found her waterproof journal and pen. Leaning up against the wall of the shelter, she turned to the first blank page of her journal and began to write. The pen felt foreign in her hand. It had been many days since she'd last held one. She stared at the blank pages and considered writing a memoir about her trip, but no words came forth. She sat back against the wall and listened to the *ta-ta-ta* of the rain hitting the tin roof. When her father died, Alex coped by ignoring the pain. She kept herself busy and involved in a million activities so that she never had to wonder or think about him. This was infinitely harder. Now she was allowing herself the space to think, to grieve, and to heal and it was proving far more difficult. So, she did the only thing she could think of. She wrote a letter to Cate to help bridge the gap between them.

CHAPTER 2

August 13, 2014 9:58 p.m.
Somewhere in Massachusetts

*D*ear Cate:

I'm not sure if I'll ever have the courage to send you this letter. It has been many months since I've written anything, let alone a letter to you. Tomorrow will be my seventy-sixth day on the Appalachian Trail. I've covered almost 700 miles on foot all by myself, including the hundred-mile wilderness in Maine and tackling New Hampshire without killing myself. In all those months, I carried around a journal and never wrote a word. Tonight is the first time I've written, and it's no surprise that my first words are for you.

When I was in college, I used to write all the time. As an English major at Amherst, I dreamed of writing the next great American novel. I faithfully wrote down my hopes and dreams. Then somewhere along the line, I met you, and everything I wrote from that point on was for you and no one else.

Do you remember the journal I created for you with my poems and letters and deepest desires? I gave it to you almost four months ago to show you how I felt about you and about all I thought we could become.

As I recall, we met for dinner at Once Upon A Table in Stockbridge on a day in April when springtime stretched its sticky green fingers skyward. We ordered vegetable dumplings to share that we never touched. We sat at the little table by the window. You handed the journal back as the waitress delivered our appetizer. You told me you just didn't feel the same. You told me you were nothing special and I should just move on. You told me you loved me as a friend. This, after everything we shared together. The next day, I tore that journal to shreds, page by page, and dumped everything unceremoniously into the garbage. That's when I decided to leave my life and hike the Appalachian Trail. You're not the only one who knows how to pick up and leave a place.

Today is a different day and a good deal of time has passed since then although my feelings have not lessened. Here I am sitting in a shelter and leaning against the wooden wall as I listen to the rain dance on the tin roof. For just a moment, you are here with me. But then a cool breeze pushes in raindrops from outside, and I shut it down. I have learned to bury the part of me that loves you. I have found a way to survive without you in my life the way I dreamed. I realize now that I am not happy and that these months have passed slowly.

You should know something: you are still the last thing I think of before I fall asleep and the first thought on my mind when I wake each morning. That has never stopped as much as I have tried and no matter how many miles I walk each day.

I took out the photo of you I carry in my backpack, and I spent a long time looking at it—at you and your golden curly hair that seems to radiate light from within. I realized yesterday how good I have become at blocking my own instincts and feelings. The thought occurred to me that I no longer trust myself. That is a problem I need to figure out how to fix, but God knows I miss you.

Today was rainy and cool here in my home state of Massachusetts. As I write, the heavy summer rain grows louder and more insistent on the tin roof of the shelter, drowning out almost all other sound in the woods. I know that if you were here with me, we'd lie together and just listen to the sound and the patterns between the raindrops. We are such similar creatures you and me. In so many ways we see the world the same, and in so many ways we are different. I wonder if you are painting now. I wish you could see some of the views I've seen. You'd want to make art after seeing them all.

I try to take each day in the present now. I try not to dream too much of kissing you. It hurts too much.

At the end of my life when I am asked about my regrets, I hope that I don't say your name. I hope that time will change things and one day we will be together. I am forever yours even if I never see your face again.

Perhaps one day I will begin to trust myself again, but right now, I don't. My heart led me to you and that caused me incredible suffering like I have never known in my life. I've always been a certain person, assured, sure of my direction. Then I met you, and everything turned on its side. You blew into my life like a warm summer breeze, then you disappeared. Now I no longer trust my instincts. I felt something real, and I had to bury it. I hope one day I find the strength to let you go.

I told you the truth, and I let it out and you ran. Someday I hope you see what kind of love it took for me to do this. I hope you see that in letting you go, I gave you the greatest gift I had to give. I gave you my heart and let you break it.

Cate, you may wonder why I continue to think about us in this way. I don't know the answer. I truly don't. I wish I didn't. In so many ways, I wish I had never met you. But in so many other ways, I know that my life has been forever changed because you came into it.

Always,

Alex

CHAPTER 3

CATE

August 2014
Provincetown, Massachusetts

Two hundred and sixty miles away at the same time, Cate sat on a driftwood tripod bench bleached white and smooth by the sun. Surrounded by art supplies on the small porch of a cabin in the bluffs of Race Point in Provincetown, she stared at a blank canvas. Her canvas, white and unblinking stared back at her as if to say, "Listen you're the painter, I'm just the blank slate." The sun was incredibly hot already and it was only seven in the morning. The light had been perfect at sunrise across the wide swath of sand stretching far off into the distance but all Cate could do was stare out as the tide rolled in with its heavy undercurrent tugging at the sharp blue sky of the midsummer horizon.

She had begun her residency stay through the Provincetown Community Compact at one of the famed rustic dune shacks in Provincetown a week ago at the beginning of August. The Compact was a nonprofit organization that maintained and stewarded two dune shacks and offered them by lottery to artists and writers for creative solitude in the pristine environment of the dunes. She'd been lucky enough to receive a three-week artist residency at the C-Scape Dune Shack, a one-and-a-half story, three-room structure that included a separate studio. She had two weeks remaining in her residency and all she had to show for it was a few sketches and one ridiculously amateurish painting. Even though the ocean was a wide expanse in front of her, she felt landlocked because she could not sail away into the great blue beyond. These were the moments she missed her parents and the gypsy sailing life they once shared.

Cate always had the uncanny ability to make any place feel like home in a matter of minutes. She had only two personal belongings that meant something to her: one was a photo of her parents and her seafaring cat Magellan hanging utterly content in her arms as they all stood smiling and laughing from atop their beloved thirty-nine-foot Southern Cross named *Cobalt Blue*. She was thirteen years old in the photo with white-blond curly hair and piercing blue eyes. A Greek sailor had taken the photo for them. The second was a simple linen scarf her mother had bought for her when they were stopped for a few weeks in Portofino, Italy. It was a gift for her fifteenth birthday and they had splurged for dinner at a fancy restaurant overlooking the Mediterranean Sea where lemon trees entwined across the entire ceiling of the terraced restaurant.

Cate took the paints, blank canvas, and easel inside the house to a little room that was used as a studio for the artists in residence. Well, house was a generous term. It was a shack. With no electricity, no running water, and no indoor plumbing, the shack was a rustic cabin perched atop a bluff in the wide expanse of the Cape Cod National Seashore dunes. Brothers Albert and Edward Noones of Cape End Motors began the dwelling in 1937. The painter Jean Cohen owned it until 1979 and moved it to a more protected location within the dunes during his ownership. Many other notable artists used it over the years adding to the energy and charm of the place. Running water came from the spring pump just down the sand dune and was carted up in big plastic canisters. The surprisingly clean and comfortable outhouse with the half-moon-shaped cutout on the door stood just thirty or so feet away. She brought camping gear like a sun shower bag and sleeping bag as well as a lot of nonperishable food and a few bottles of wine. If she needed something, she could walk through the dunes into downtown Provincetown before the sun rose high on the horizon. The walk took about an hour and she could usually manage a ride back with one of the Art's Dune Tours guides, but she enjoyed the peace and solitude of the shack compared to the partying summer bustle of town.

The austere surroundings of the shack weren't new to her. Living on a sailboat all those years was similar: confining spaces, little technology, and only the essentials. She had her paints and her view of the ocean. At night, kerosene lanterns illuminated the whitewashed walls and worn wooden floors, casting a comforting glow that felt otherworldly and reminded Cate of nights aboard a sailboat. In fact, every time Cate looked around the cabin day or night, she was struck by how the simple, mismatched surroundings of a random chair or table fit together so perfectly with the sea and sand and sun outside. A constant breeze puffed through every window so the air was always fresh and salty. She didn't even have much cell phone reception here. In the past, this kind of life worked fine for her, but not any longer. Something heavy had shifted within her altering her ability to easily move from place to place. No matter how much she wanted to love where she was because it was so tranquil and perfect, she couldn't. The hole in her heart wouldn't allow it.

Cate flopped down on the flimsy mattress covered by her light sleeping bag. It was too hot to paint outside right now anyway. If she felt productive she could go into the studio room and finish any number of things she had half-started. Or, she could take a nap or go for a swim. Unable to make a decision, she just lay in bed, staring up at the rustic wooden ceiling of the shack and feeling the cool ocean breeze flow through the window just above her head. She closed her eyes and was immediately transported back to a moment with Alex when they first kissed.

Both of them were tipsy from tequila. It was the first time Alex visited her in her rented loft apartment a couple of weeks after they first met at school. Cate invited her there after running out on her when they first met for drinks. She hadn't meant to simply take off and leave Alex but her head had buzzed with the faint pressure of something tiny and barely noticeable tying and binding her to Alex with little silken spider web threads. The feeling made her queasy and uncertain and so she ran away. But after taking a week to mull over her sudden departure, she was tired of getting the cold shoulder from Alex at school. It was clear she had hurt and confused Alex and she wanted desperately to make it right. So, she put on her big girl pants and invited Alex to her apartment.

Cate needed to be alone with her to determine if the pull she felt toward Alex deep inside was real or imaginary. She'd had plenty of lovers before but she always held them in a space of her own creation that was one step away from commitment and one step away from departure. There, in that in-between zone, was the only place where she felt comfortable with another person because she always had one foot out the door, and above all, she always had control. Allowing someone to truly care for her held her back and kept her from moving on to the next place or the next experience and that was never acceptable. Freedom was her only true and permanent lover by choice.

She remembered smelling Alex's perfume when she walked into her apartment and the way Alex's long dark hair had shone in the light of her doorway. Alex was hesitant and on guard after Cate's great disappearing act at Webster's. Even the way Alex moved was sensual before Cate was even fully aware of it. The pull was immediate and every little tilt of Alex's head or fleeting change in expression intoxicated Cate.

When Alex arrived, she saw Cate's artwork all over the loft and was curious to see it. At first Cate was shy to show her work to Alex because she did not want to feel judged or appraised by any of it. She was not the sum of the brushstrokes surely as a writer was not the sum of the words she put on a page. But on the other hand, she wanted desperately for Alex to see her artwork because it provided a window to deep inside her soul and she needed Alex to see that part of her.

Alex took her time looking carefully at all of her paintings that either hung on the exposed brick walls of the loft or were stacked on the floor. She took great care to observe them individually and asked Cate several questions like what she was thinking when she painted something or where she felt her creativity for a specific piece came from. All of Alex's questions showed a caring and unique ability to cut to the heart of a piece of art and see it for what it really was each and every time. Her innate ability to see beyond the paint on canvas to the ultimate meaning behind the pieces only made her more appealing.

Cate found herself watching Alex closely: the way she crossed a leg or the way she leaned forward when Cate said something she found intriguing. All of it ignited something within Cate that had been dormant for a long, long time.

Hours later, exhausted by all the conversation, they had lain on Cate's mattress in the middle of the floor drinking tequila as soft jazz played in the background. Cate remembered how Alex was sprawled on her bed with one arm over her head, propped up on pillows facing her. She wore a black T-shirt and jeans and was barefoot with her toes painted a shimmery pink.

Cate still didn't know why she did it, but she had rolled up one of Alex's pant legs to the midcalf and poured a little tequila on her bare skin. She remembered how smooth and strong Alex's leg was as her wet hand ran up and down Alex's calf. Alex laughed and sat up. Cate bent toward her and saw how the light shone in Alex's long dark hair. The energy between them had buzzed all night and now as they moved closer together, Cate felt the electricity passing back and forth between them like a secret, hidden stream of white lightning. One of Alex's hands rested on Cate's thigh and the other moved up to brush away stray curls from Cate's face. The sheer act was so gentle, Cate shuddered at the memory of it. Of all the things they shared together over the following months, there was something magical and intensely personal about the way Alex always reverently moved Cate's hair away before she kissed her. It was, perhaps, the one thing Cate missed the most amidst a wide variety of memories to choose from.

Moments before their lips touched for the first time, Cate remembered saying over and over again, "This is for you." To this day she had no idea why she said that. At first, she chalked it up to being drunk but the more she thought back to that night, the more she wondered why she felt like kissing Alex was an incredibly beautiful and gentle gift she could give her. Their kiss was like a homecoming for Cate. It started out soft and delicate then shifted into a heated, passionate embrace within a few moments.

The sheer craving inside the memory overwhelmed Cate so much that she jolted upright in her tiny dune shack bed, beads of sweat sliding between her breasts down to her navel. Cate yanked off her tank top and caressed her own body, trying to remember Alex's touch. Try as she might, she couldn't replicate the singular feeling of Alex's hands upon her so she stopped. There wasn't any use trying to masturbate when nothing came close to the feeling of Alex's body or hands on her. She thought about finding a lover even for a one-night stand, but the mere thought of someone else's hands upon her made her cringe. She was perfectly clear about who she wanted touching her, but the problem was that woman was nowhere in sight and might never be again.

Cate rose from the bed and began pacing around the shack. She had no need to put her shirt back on. It wasn't like anyone

would bother her here. As she paced back and forth, she tried to
stop the thoughts from racing around inside her head. She knew
there was something wrong with her. No one had ever gotten into
her head like this. She couldn't take a step without thinking of
Alex in one way or another and it infuriated her. She felt weak.
She felt as though she'd lost control. She was in the middle of a
full-blown mutiny with her own mind and her own heart. It was
as if her thoughts were no longer her own and neither was her
body. How could she let things go this far? How could she have
been so stupid to think she could just shut off the spigot and walk
away? Feeling as though she might explode, she ran, still topless,
from the shack, out the green door, down the few steps of the
deck, and onto the sand path. She half slid, half walked with wide
gaping steps down the face of the huge dune to the ocean where
she ran to the water and dove in.

Race Point sat on the Atlantic side of Provincetown and as
such, the water even in the heat of summer was always chilly. The
cold water sent shockwaves through her body but it made her feel
alive. She looked up and saw several seals with their heads
bobbing up and down from wave to wave watching her swim.
While the water was cold on one side, the hot summer sun
warmed her on the other. After a few minutes of floating effortlessly, careful not to be dragged too far by the undertow, she
swam to shore and rested in the hot sand to dry off. Her sun-
bleached hair was so long it covered her breasts completely and
she laughed at what she must look like—half mermaid,
half human.

She decided to begin writing Alex letters. She couldn't bring
herself to call her yet or see her, but she could write to Alex about
what she thought and her decisions in the hopes she could make
Alex see she was trying to open herself up. Alex had opened her
heart to Cate and poured out her feelings in a beautifully written
journal. The depth of emotions terrified Cate as she leafed
through the journal while they sat inside one of Alex's favorite

restaurants. Cate's knee-jerk response was to run as fast as she could in the other direction. She told Alex she wasn't in love with her. She said they should be friends, then handed the journal back to Alex even though every cell in her body wanted to embrace Alex and thank her for creating such an exquisite gift. And as she dropped the journal with a thud on the table, she saw the light go out in Alex's eyes. It was almost more than she could bear. She packed that night. She dropped all her artwork off at a local consignment shop, quit her job as art teacher at Burr Elementary as suddenly as she took it, and drove back to the only home she'd ever known. She ended up back in New Haven, crashing with an acquaintance from Yale and working as a barista at a gourmet coffee shop until her residency started. Now as she lay on the beach at what felt like the end of the earth, all she had to settle her were memories. If she wasn't in the right mind-set to paint, she would write. Maybe then Alex could feel the love she had in her heart. Maybe then she could retake control of her own self again and begin to feel like something more than an empty shell strewn ashore by the incoming tide.

CHAPTER 4

August 17, 2014 1:14 p.m.
Provincetown, Massachusetts

*D*ear Alex:
　　You told me once that I didn't bare my soul to you. You said I kept my heart locked up in a box and was unwilling to share it with you or anyone. You said I loved my freedom more than I would ever love you. I'm in Provincetown inside a rustic little dune shack. It's too bright and hot outside to paint. I hate writing letters, but I am trying. God knows I am trying to make you understand leaving will always keep me coming back.

It's been exactly 104 days since we stopped talking. I know this because every day has been a test of wills for me, so much so that I've kept track. I broke your heart on May 5. It was a Monday and we met at that cute little restaurant you loved so much. It was there I told you I didn't love you. I lied of course. You are normally so astute. How you didn't see that I was lying is still a mystery to me.

I wish I were on a boat watching the clouds slide across the sky as the wind fills my sails and the cold salt spray hits my face reminding me I'm alive. The sea is constant and flowing. No mistake ever seems permanent or too big to fix when you're on the water. Everything has a solution. Time will make it so, but not this time.

Alex, I'm afraid of loving you. What if I love you too much and you leave? What if you make me stay in one place and my soul turns all gray and brittle and disintegrates? What would I do if you asked me to choose between loving you and feeling carefree? I couldn't take that chance so I did what I always did: I shut things down before you asked.

How can I possibly explain to you the love I have for you? Maybe I could paint it in the orange-red-stained hue of a sunset on Race Point when even the seagulls are joyous in the spectrum of light and air and sand. Maybe I could show you that inside, the shifting of blue to green on a palette is merely a reflection of what I feel for you inside.

Mercury is in retrograde. Apparently this means I might be haunted by my past. I'm not sure haunted is the right word. And I'd like to think I've changed in the 104 days since I've heard your voice but I'm not sure I have. I'd like to think I am beyond that awful time when you hurled hurtful words at me with venom. I may be beyond it, but the scar hurts— especially on days like this when I am particularly at your mercy and the heat of the sun turns all my scars pink and tender anyway.

Don't give up on me. I'm trying to find my way back to you.

Love,

Cate

CHAPTER 5

ALEX

January 2014, seven months earlier
Stockbridge, Massachusetts

Seven months before hiking the Appalachian Trail was even on Alex's radar, she had just returned to work after the extended holiday break. Late in the afternoon when she had a free period, she heard laughter down a wing that was usually eerily silent. Curious, she decided to check it out. She had a period to kill before lunch anyway. Her steps echoed down the empty tiled hallway toward the art studio where ancient Mrs. Critchley taught for thirty years before retiring at the end of the calendar year due to her husband's ailing health. Mrs. Critchley was a fixture in the elementary school Alex taught in. Alex never could understand how someone who looked so imposing and stern and seemed to be 400 years old taught an activity as fun as art. All the teachers stayed away from the old, crabby woman. She was tough as nails with her fellow staff as well as with her students. Hence the perennial lack of laughter down this particular wing of the school.

Today was different. A new substitute teacher had just taken over for the remaining five months of the school year. After that, the Board would vote in a permanent replacement. The laughter coming from the art room was infectious, and Alex smiled before she even peeked into the room. As she walked down the hall, her eyes wandered to the windows and a postcard view of light snow falling. While they hadn't had many snow day setbacks thus far this winter, several snowstorms had blown through during the recent holiday break, covering everything in white. Alex wrapped her cardigan tighter around herself as she walked down the hall.

A few moments later, Alex looked into art room 504 to see a drop-dead beautiful woman with flowing blond curly hair and flashing blue eyes wielding a paintbrush. Alex was so used to seeing Mrs. Critchley in her starched collars and drab dresses that the sight of this young, vibrant woman was jarring. The woman stood at the front of the class barefoot, wearing paint-stained cargo pants rolled midcalf and a Def Leppard tank top, despite the winter chill in the air. She was tall and athletic and even a little tan for this early January day. The kids watched their new teacher with rapt fascination. They were all working together on a giant sheet of paper that stretched the entire length of the classroom. The desks and worktables were stacked in the back of the room, and the kids had stretched out on the floor with paints, legs, and elbows everywhere.

"Don't look at me to tell you what to create. Close your eyes and make whatever you see in your mind!"

"Anything?" a little boy named Artis said incredulously.

"Anything!"

"But I see a fuzzy monster eating a chocolate-chip cookie!" yelled Rachel, a cute little girl with fiery-red hair.

"Then paint that!" said the new teacher who lit up the room with her ridiculously bright smile.

Alex felt herself being pulled into the room by the woman's energy and that megawatt smile. A moment later, the woman turned and saw her. Alex stood there staring at the most incredible blue eyes she had ever seen: it was as if they reflected an early summer sky and the rays of the sun. Suddenly one of Alex's students Jessica yelled, "Ms. McKenzie! What are *you* doing here?"

Alex was shaken from her reverie, and for a moment, she couldn't speak. Finally, the woman turned her head back to the little girl, and the spell was broken. "Hi, Rachel. I thought I'd check in to see how you were all liking your new art teacher."

"OMG, Ms. McKenzie, she is like the most awesome teacher ever in the whole world. Um, I mean after you," said David, waving a paint-soaked brush in the air, spattering paint in all directions.

Alex laughed. The woman laughed, and all Alex could think of was sleigh bells at Christmas.

"Well, thanks for checking up on us," the woman said kindly to Alex. "I think we've managed to go through most of the paint left in storage." She shifted her attention back to the kids. "Time to clean up, my little artists. Go rinse your brushes and bring all the paints up to me, please. We'll continue working on this master-piece tomorrow." The kids jumped up in a flurry of activity, giving Alex a moment to make an introduction.

"Hi there. I'm..."

"Ms. McKenzie," said the woman, wiping paint off her hands with a rag.

"Right. Alex actually."

"Hi, Alex. I'm Ms. Conrad, but you can call me Cate." Cate held up her paint-covered hands. "I'd shake your hand, but I'm a little messy right about now."

Again, Cate threw Alex that smile. Alex's mouth was suddenly Mojave Desert dry. She tried to talk, but no sound came out. She nodded and smiled awkwardly. A few moments passed, and Alex became acutely embarrassed and aware Cate was watching her. She knew she was making a total idiot of herself. Alex waved and bolted off down the hallway. She made a beeline for the teacher's bathroom and locked the door behind her. Her palms were sweaty. She stared at herself in the mirror and saw her face deep red in a full-on blush. Alex splashed water on her face and drank a few sips from her hand. She steadied her body against the sink for a couple of moments. The last time she'd blushed like this was in her sophomore year of college when Isabel Feliciano kissed her in front of everyone at the soccer house party. Back then, she'd had a visceral, potent, physical reaction to a new person in the most unlikely of places. Once again, Alex was thrown off kilter, here of all places, too. School was always a haven for her, a place where she was in total control. She unlocked the door to the bathroom and peered down the hallway to make sure the coast was clear. Then she rushed back to the relative safety of her classroom and wondered when she would see Cate again and what her story was. It was as if a bright light had been turned on in the darkness and all Alex wanted to do was walk toward the light.

CHAPTER 6

A few days after that embarrassing initial meeting with Cate, Alex's head remained buried in stories her fifth-grade class wrote after reading *Alexander and the Terrible, Horrible, Not Good, Very Bad Day* aloud. She had asked them to use their imaginations and create a day like Alexander's but pretend it happened to them. They were tasked with including what happened, how they felt, and how their families reacted. This was one of her favorite lessons, especially since *Alexander* was one of her favorite books. But it also gave her insights about her students. Oftentimes they wrote about things really happening at home, like divorce or family illness, and these details helped her gain a better understanding of their lives and any issues they were dealing with outside the classroom.

Alex was reading Kellie DiLauro's story about how her dog died, which she knew had recently happened in the little girl's life. The girl's mother Angela—one of Alex's favorites—had sent her a note alerting her to the family's loss and how devastated Kellie was to lose her best friend. As Alex read the little girl's description of her dog Bowser leaving them for heaven, tears streamed down her face. She didn't hear the light knock at her doorway and she never heard anyone enter her classroom. Since the school day and week were over, the hallways were quiet.

"You're crying," a gentle woman's voice said, startling Alex out of the sad story and into the present. She looked up to see the mass of curly blond hair and Cate's kind eyes looking down at her. Alex quickly wiped the tears away and began cleaning up her cluttered desk.

"Oh, hi. I never heard you come in. I was so engrossed in Kellie's terrible day story. Her dog Bowser died."

"Why not have them write happy stories?" asked Cate, her head tilted to one side.

"We do that too, but we just read this book about a really bad day and it's a great way for me to learn more about their lives." Alex paused for a moment, unsure of what to say next. She felt the blush rising again in her cheeks and took a swig from her water bottle to quell it. If Cate noticed, she didn't let on.

"I just stopped by to see if you were available for coffee or a drink or something. I haven't made any new friends here at school. I get the sense the last teacher wasn't all that, well, social, and it feels like everyone is giving me a wide berth." Cate laughed and the bubbly, melodious sound again caught Alex off guard.

"Well, let's see. The day is over. The week is over. I've been reading sad stories written by my fifth-grade students. I think happy hour is in order. How about Webster's?"

"Of course, the English teacher would pick the place that has books everywhere and is named after a dictionary."

Alex laughed. "That and they make a great margarita."

"Sold. I'll see you there around five thirty?" responded Cate.

"Perfect. See you then."

Alex looked down at her outfit and realized she didn't have much time to shower and change. And she had to change. The thought suddenly occurred to her: this wasn't a date. This was just another coworker inviting her out for a drink so she could make friends at work. This wasn't a date.

All the way home Alex kept telling herself this wasn't a date over and over again but she still felt butterflies in her stomach and she still felt like it *was* a date. She had no idea if Cate was gay or not and she had been single for long enough to realize her game was dormant, if not nonexistent.

∾

At precisely five thirty, Alex walked into Webster's, one of her favorite local bars. She didn't want to seem too dressed for the meeting so she ultimately decided on her favorite pair of boyfriend jeans and a white button-down shirt and her favorite tan cashmere cardigan. Her outfit might have been a little preppy, but it was unassuming and comfortable. The local hangout was named for Noah Webster, the nineteenth-century genius who first developed a comprehensive dictionary after decades of research. The place was much as you'd expect it to be: comfortable chairs, a dark mahogany bar, old books on every subject imaginable lining each and every wall. Even the bill was delivered in a hollowed-out Webster's dictionary. It took a moment for Alex's eyes to adjust to the shadowy light inside, but after a few turns around the bar, she spotted Cate across the room sitting in a plush lounge chair. Cate was bent over the small side table deep in concentration. As Alex approached, she saw that Cate was sketching an unsuspecting older man seated across from the bar on a cocktail napkin.

"Always the artist I see," said Alex as she took the seat to Cate's left. Cate looked up and smiled broadly. Again, Alex felt her stomach flip. *This is not a date* she reminded herself.

"Hey there! I was just passing time. I got here a few minutes early."

Alex picked up the cocktail napkin and inspected it, comparing it to the man across the room. "Wow. This is fantastic. You truly captured him—his essence I mean."

"Well, thanks. Now I'm blushing." Cate smiled, clearly alluding to Alex's previous blush-fests at their last meetings.

Thankfully, the waitress saved Alex by taking their margarita and flatbread orders. Alex was momentarily frozen, uncertain of what to say next. She was acutely aware of the jazz music playing in the background and the laughter from the bar. They sat in silence for a few awkward moments. Alex made a conscious effort not to fidget in her seat.

Cate thankfully broke the ice once again. "So how long have you been teaching at Burr Elementary?" She leaned back in the oversized armchair and crossed her slender legs.

"Let's see, I've been there for nine years, since 2005. I waited tables until there was an opening the following school year after I finished my master's degree in 2004. The previous English teacher had taken maternity leave but decided not to return." Alex kept her hand wrapped around her margarita glass trying to mentally transfer the melting ice to her burning cheeks.

"And how do you like it at Burr? It seems like a cool place." Cate leaned forward with interest as she munched on a piece of flatbread.

"I love it there. I'm allowed to be creative with my curriculum and I feel supported by the administration, which is a huge blessing." Alex sipped her drink, and looked at Cate. She noticed how blond Cate's long eyelashes were. She had never seen eyelashes that long and that blond. Alex had this sudden thought of Cate giving her a butterfly kiss on her stomach with those incredible eyelashes as they lay naked in bed. Instantly, she sucked her sip of margarita down the wrong way. Alex barely managed to put her drink down before succumbing to fits of coughing.

"Are you okay?" Cate jumped up from her chair and smacked Alex on the back hard enough to jolt her out of her coughing outburst. Her hand rested gently on Alex's shoulder and the heat from her touch was like a slow, comforting burn.

"I'm fine," Alex squeaked out, covering her entire face with a napkin. *This is not a good look* was all she could think of. Cate stared at her with concern, her hand still firmly in place. "Really. I'm okay. Thanks. It just went down the wrong pipe." Alex smoothed her hair and took a deep gulp of air. When Cate removed her hand and sat back down, Alex felt the coolness return to her skin.

"Sorry about that. So, how long have you been teaching art?" Alex tried desperately to move the attention away from her and onto Cate. Cate sipped her drink.

"This is my first time. I'm not really a teacher. I'm an artist but I needed the money and started looking at other options. The idea of doing something other than art to pay the bills was awful to me so I decided to look at jobs where I could still be involved in creating art in some way. Plus, I love kids so I gave it a shot." Cate ran her fingers through her long hair, brushing a stray curl from her face.

"Well, talk about being in the right place at the right time. Your predecessor Mrs. Critchley was at Burr Elementary forever. Not to mention she was a tough old bird. I'm sure you've been like a breath of fresh air for the kids."

Cate smiled in a way that lit up the entire room. "I heard stories about Mrs. Critchley and none of them were flattering."

Alex laughed. "Yeah, she is the stuff of legend. So, have they told you if they'll make it permanent?"

"Oh, I don't want anything permanent. I'm happy to do this until the end of the school year but I don't want to be tied down to anything. I can't be tied down. Plus, I've got an upcoming residency in a Provincetown, Massachusetts dune shack this summer. Cate nonchalantly brushed some stray crumbs off her leg.

"Wow. That's incredible. What kind of art do you specialize in? Is that even the right question? I know next to nothing about art," Alex said, fidgeting.

"Sure, it is. I'm not an expert in anything yet but I studied art at Yale and stayed on for an MFA in painting and printmaking.

I'm still exploring creatively, but I guess I'd say I lean more toward Expressionism."

"I have absolutely no idea what Expressionism is," admitted Alex shyly.

"It's a relatively modern movement that started mostly in Germany where the art is charged with an emotional and spiritual vision of the world. Van Gogh was an Expressionist. It's all about exploring the inner landscape of the soul."

Alex swallowed the rest of her drink. "Holy crap. You're like scary smart, aren't you? We can't be friends." The words slipped out before Alex could stop them. The moment the last sentence left her lips she wished she could take it all back. The last thing she wanted to do was present herself as the idiot English teacher. Again, Alex blushed. Again, Alex was sure Cate saw it.

Cate laughed at the remark. "You're funny. Like the kind of funny where you don't realize how funny you are, and that makes you funnier." Her eyes twinkled. "I think I need another margarita. How about you?"

"Sure, why not? I've already made a fool of myself twice." Alex held up her empty glass to get the waitress's attention. "So how did you know you wanted to be an artist," she asked in between bites of grilled flatbread.

"Always I guess. My parents were, I mean are, very unusual." Alex laughed at that.

"What's so funny?" Cate asked.

"My mother would kill me if I ever told someone she was unusual."

"Well mine definitely are." Cate smiled. "When I was five they sold their house in Vermont and bought a big, beautiful sailboat with plans to circumnavigate. They said they wanted to experience life instead of being passive participants in it."

Alex shifted in her chair and leaned in closer. A few people at the bar were making a lot of noise and Alex wanted to be sure she heard Cate's every word. "They both must've had great jobs to travel like that."

"They're artists too, both painters," Cate said.

The waitress delivered their second round of margaritas. Alex handed the waitress their empty plates and glasses to speed up her departure. She was enthralled by Cate's story. "Did you really live on a boat?"

"For a long time, yeah." Cate sipped her fresh drink. "We spent the next twelve years living on that boat as we sailed all around the world together."

"But what about school?" Alex asked, her eyes wide.

"My mom homeschooled me and we painted every day. They sold their art in ports everywhere, which easily paid for our modest life at sea. Each day was an entirely different view. It was an amazing way to grow up that I wouldn't trade for the world." She grinned. "Actually, my first week at Yale was the first time I spent more than a day on dry land in years. I remember I couldn't sleep for a week."

Alex was spellbound. "Hence your disdain for being tied down," she mused, almost to herself.

Cate looked confused for a moment. "Oh, right. Yes, I did say that. Exactly. The idea of being in once place for my entire life just doesn't appeal to me. Once a vagabond always a vagabond."

"That concept is totally foreign to me, but it sounds amazing." Alex chuckled. "Moving around like you did is unusual to most people."

Alex looked around the familiar bar. "I was born right here in Stockbridge. My mom lives in the same house my sister and I were born in. In fact, she was born in that house too. We lived there my entire life, even while my father was stationed at Hanscom Air Force Base outside of Boston.

"Ah, so you're an army brat?" Cate's eyes sparkled. "You must've moved around some then?"

"Not really. Air Force." Alex stiffened as she mentioned her father. "My dad was a Lieutenant Colonel in the 66th Air Base Group. We were lucky because we didn't move around at all. My dad lived on base during the week and came home on weekends and worked there from before I was born." She added softly, "He died in a training accident when I was ten years old."

"Oh, I'm so sorry. That must've been awful." Cate leaned forward and gently rested her hand on Alex's knee.

Alex relaxed at her touch and continued. "It was awful. My dad had this larger-than-life personality. Everyone loved him. He was strict but fair, and he was always so much fun to be around." Alex was silent for a moment as she tried not to let too much emotion sneak out. It never got easier to talk about her dad, no matter how much time had passed. She shifted the subject and tried to perk up the suddenly flagging conversation. "Anyway, I went to college at Amherst and have only done some summer vacation traveling to all the usual places like Gettysburg and Disney World. As soon as I landed the job at Burr, I bought a little Cape around the corner from my sister, and I've been there ever since."

"Well your dad sounds like he was an amazing man. I can't even imagine what my life would be like without my dad. He's always been so steady and calm." Cate's eyes were firmly on Alex's. After a few moments, she broke eye contact and took a sip of her drink. "And being here your whole life doesn't really have too many downsides. Sometimes I wish I had a place that I could call home like that."

"How did you end up here in Stockbridge anyway? We're not exactly on the main line to anywhere," said Alex. "Especially not for sailboats!"

"True." Cate laughed. "There are two reasons. First, my parents had given me a gift certificate for a 'Drawing Closer to Nature' course at the Kripalu Institute that lasted a week."

"I love that place. It's so peaceful and serene," Alex interjected.

"It is." Cate continued, "I fell in love with the Berkshires. After the course ended, I wanted to check out the Norman Rockwell

Museum and wound up loving it here so much I decided to stay for a while. I got a great deal to rent an old warehouse loft with perfect light."

"Just like that? You decided to pick up and move to a place because you visited it and liked it?" Alex asked, looking at Cate in surprise.

Cate laughed. "Yep. Just like that. It's kind of how I live my life actually. I go wherever the mood strikes me." She waved her hand around like she had a magic wand that could take her anywhere she wanted to go.

"That sounds amazing...and very brave. I'm much more of a planner and a plotter," Alex disclosed to her.

"Of course. The English teacher would love a good plot." Cate winked.

"Touché." Alex smiled. She leaned in and rested her hand on Cate's knee. "I don't know why but I feel like we've known each other for a long time. Like we're just catching up or something."

Cate looked surprised by Alex's comment. She didn't respond, but tilted her head and continued staring at Alex. Alex was taken totally off guard not only because she had just shared that intensely private thought with Cate out loud, but also because Cate had yet to say anything in return. Alex immediately regretted the statement and quickly pulled her hand off Cate's knee. She was suddenly worried she'd made Cate uncomfortable. At the very least she had made herself uncomfortable.

"I'm so sorry, I didn't mean to...I mean, I wasn't trying to imply...Oh for cripes sakes. I'm an idiot. Just ignore I said that. You probably think I'm a new age wing nut or something. I didn't mean to..." Alex stammered nearly to the point of incoherence.

Again, Cate put her hand on Alex's shoulder, and Alex immediately quieted. "Alex. Stop. It's okay. I understood what you meant. I was just surprised you said it because, at that moment, I felt exactly the same thing. I don't believe in accidents. I think everything happens for a reason. There was a reason why I came here to Stockbridge and started teaching at your school. Maybe that reason was meeting you." In one swift motion, Cate lowered her hand to Alex's lap where their hands met. Alex squeezed Cate's hand involuntarily and looked down, noticing how square and strong Cate's hand looked in hers.

Somewhere along the line, the "this is not a date" mantra Alex had been repeating went by the wayside. This was feeling more and more like a date, a good date. Like the best first date ever kind of date. She wasn't imagining it; Cate was flirting with her. Alex never got this kind of vibe with any of her friends or coworkers. Actually, come to think of it, Alex never got this strong a vibe from anyone, even the other women she had dated in the past. Nothing came close to this odd sensation of warmth and butterflies and recognition all at once. It felt as if every cell in her body was more attuned, more alive, and leaning ever so slightly in the direction of Cate.

Cate finally pulled her hand away and Alex felt as if a cloud had just passed in front of the sun. She looked at Cate and couldn't quite place the expression on her face. All of the warmth Cate had just exhibited was somehow suddenly boxed up. Cate suddenly rose from her seat and grabbed her bag, digging around inside it only to drop money on the table. "I'm so sorry. I just realized what time it is. I really have to go. See you at school Monday?"

"Um, sure," said an utterly perplexed Alex, but Cate had already disappeared. Dazed, Alex tried to regain her focus and her footing.

CHAPTER 7

August 2014
Appalachian Trail at Sage's Ravine, Massachusetts

*I*n the early morning hours, seven months later, Alex allowed herself a few extra minutes in her warm sleeping bag as the sun rose all warm and golden yellow to the East. This was her favorite time of day, when her mind straddled consciousness and unconsciousness, dreams and the day ahead. It was always as if those moments held out the air of pure and total hope that anything was possible because she was dreaming and living simultaneously.

The birds began their morning activity and their early morning songs circled the shelter. There was no schedule on the Trail, and that was sheer beauty. There was no alarm clock. She was her own master with no one and nothing to answer to. Admittedly, that freedom scared her at first. She was such a routine-oriented person that having the vast expanse of space and time in front of her was overwhelming. Now Alex reveled in these tiny, seemingly insignificant moments that had a way of sliding across the surface of her consciousness like ripples on a cool, clear lake.

She knew that in a matter of minutes she would be packed and on her way for the day, but for now there was no rush. There was just this place and her breath and the birds around her. She closed her eyes and the thought of kissing Cate silently crept into her mind, kidnapping her thoughts of peace and quiet. Alone in the shelter, she allowed the butterflies in her stomach to fly free at the mere thought of Cate's lips on hers. And for a moment, the freedom to imagine and pretend, the liberty to wish and to dream, was granted as she drifted back off to that place of sleeping and not sleeping. Even though she had not seen Cate in four months, it all still felt so close to her, so raw and tender. Suddenly a chipmunk sounded an alarm chirp so loud Alex jumped up as if smacked awake by a frying pan.

"I'm up, I'm up," she grumbled to the chipmunk who sat up on two feet eating an acorn and staring at her from the entrance of the shelter.

Twenty minutes later, she stood at the base of Sage's Ravine looking up. Getting down to this shelter last night in the pouring rain near dark was treacherous. The Ravine, named for Simeon Sage, who founded the Sage Ironworks Company in the nineteenth century, tumbled down a good thirty feet. Last night as daylight faded and the rain poured down, Alex had to lower her backpack with her rope and slide down the Ravine's side on her bottom. Today posed an entirely different challenge: climbing out when the rocks and leaves were still slick. This was when hiking poles definitely helped. She turned her torso sideways and stepped up as if she was on a hillside with skis on. After a few steps, the side of the Ravine was too steep so she shifted her poles under one arm to literally climb out with her feet and hands engaged. Once at the top, she struggled to catch her breath. This was not the way she hoped to start her day. She was muddy and wet and knew she had about an eight-mile hike until she reached Salisbury, Connecticut for a much-needed couple of nights on a real bed with a real shower and that double cheeseburger she'd been dreaming about.

As Alex hiked, her mind switched back and forth from thinking about that cheeseburger or fried chicken or an ice-cold Coca-Cola to wondering how her sister was and to thinking about that letter she wrote to Cate early yesterday morning. It was the first letter she wrote to Cate since last seeing her over four months ago. It was the first time she wrote anything at all and the idea that her first words were for Cate both angered her and calmed her at the same time. The daily struggle of loving Cate and hating that she loved her manifested itself in a surprising variety of ways.

Alex stopped for a moment to take in the beauty of Sage's Ravine from the top, now on a sunny morning. It was a spot her dad would have loved, with the Ravine tumbling down the side of forest and rock near the Massachusetts-Connecticut border. Because of the heavy overnight rain, the series of falls and cascades were loud and breathtaking. "Hey, Dad," she said aloud. "This is a pretty spot. Could you imagine taking Mom here? She'd never get out of that ravine!"

Since her father's death twenty-three years ago, it had become her special habit to talk to him as if he were right there next to her. Once her sister Sara caught her talking a mile a minute with no one around. When Sara asked to whom she was speaking, Alex had said, "Daddy. I'm telling him all about school today. He says hi by the way and that you should talk to him more."

The certainty by which Alex believed her father was there with her in spirit had never been in question or up for debate. She felt his presence everywhere. While she wasn't a big believer in ghosts, she did believe in an afterlife and in the idea that our souls move on when our bodies do not. This was one of the primary reasons why she felt so safe alone on the Appalachian Trail—a fact she couldn't explain to anyone, even her sister. Alex knew as surely as the sun rose every morning that her father would never let anything happen to her and she felt the bubble of protection surround her at every turn.

At around ten o'clock, she took a break to eat breakfast and to send her best friends Marcie and Emma a daily update that she was alive and well. It was hot today and she had already sweat through her T-shirt. She dropped her pack on a large rock and bent over to stretch her lower back. She gobbled down a protein bar and some trail mix and drank almost half a liter of water. Since there was a clear stream nearby, she took a few extra minutes to refill her water and purify it with her Steripen. The entire break lasted only fifteen or twenty minutes but on the quiet trail, it felt like much longer. After using the wilderness bathroom —the one part of her hike that her mother just could not come to terms with—she repacked her bag and expertly hoisted it back over her shoulders in one smooth motion. Her pack was pretty light right now since she had no food left except for today's lunch. Her pace quickened. The faster she made it into town, the faster she would be awarded with a shower and a burger. There was nothing quite like the incentive of a full belly to propel her down the Trail.

She hiked for the better part of four more hours with only a brief stop to finish off her trail mix and beef jerky before she reached the historic and quaint Main Street of downtown Salisbury in Litchfield County, Connecticut. Salisbury was only about a forty-minute drive from her hometown, but she had made the decision that she did not want to go home for a visit. She knew she'd be too tempted to leave the Trail for good if she slept in her own bed for even a night. She also asked that her mom and sister not visit her while she was there. They didn't like it much, but they thankfully respected her wishes.

As she walked up Main Street, Alex noticed the way people looked at her. She knew she was a mess but she had grown accustomed to the looks, and the stink no longer bothered her. She continued on about another half mile, trying to keep herself in the shade as much as possible until she reached her destination: the White Hart Inn. It was a beautiful white farmhouse with a large wraparound porch and her choice to stay here was quite a splurge for her financially. But she knew after 600 miles, hostels, motels, and shelters, this would be about the time she'd want some serious pampering. As she walked inside, she immediately felt the cool air ripple over her bare arms. She prayed no other guests arrived at the same time, afraid she'd make them run for the hills. She rang the bell at the desk and waited, taking in the charming décor and surroundings.

"Hello there. You look like you could use a shower!"

Alex jumped at the voice. It had been several days since she'd spoken to another soul.

"Oh, hi. Yes, I'm definitely in need of one," she said.

"You must be Alex McKenzie. I'm Dan, the hotel manager. You're our only thru-hiker so far. Most of the hikers prefer more budget accommodations. I believe we have a couple of packages waiting for you too." Dan disappeared behind the counter and popped back up a moment later with two large boxes. "I bet you're looking forward to what's inside those boxes!"

"I definitely am."

"Oh wait, there is one more that came in today." He dipped below the counter once again. "Ah, here it is. Your friends Marcie and Emma said this was a special delivery." He handed her the box.

Alex smiled broadly at the mere mention of her best friends.

"So, are you a Northbounder or Southbounder?"

"I'm a Southbounder," responded Alex confidently.

"Wow! Good for you. I understand that's the more difficult of the two directions," said Dan casually as he worked at the computer to check Alex in.

"Maine and New Hampshire were no picnic, that's for sure, but I survived them."

"Well, we welcome you to the White Hart Inn and are so glad you'll be staying here for three nights. Since this is a pretty quiet time of year for us, we have some extra availability so I've upgraded you to a suite in our Gideon Smith House. Continental breakfast is included and of course we have the taproom and dining room available to you as well. I see that you prepaid and we already have your credit card on record, so you are all set, Ms. McKenzie. Please let me know if there is anything I can help you with during your stay."

As Dan handed Alex her room key, she asked, "Yes there is one thing. When I made my reservations, I was told I would be able to do some laundry?"

"Oh yes, of course." Dan handed Alex a laundry bag. "Just put all your dirty clothes in here and we will take care of everything."

"Are you sure? I don't mind doing it myself. Your staff might not be able to handle it."

Dan laughed. "Don't worry, we've had a few hikers here before. We know when you mean your clothes are dirty, you mean really dirty. We'll have everything back to you first thing tomorrow morning."

"Thank you so much."

Alex grabbed her packages and headed to the Gideon Smith House toward her room.

"Wow," she said aloud as the door closed behind her. Her suite was just beautiful although everything was white so she was afraid to sit down or touch anything even though her first urge was to jump on the bed and make imaginary snow angels. One of her two boxes, called a "bounce box," contained all of the items she needed while in town but didn't want to carry. She bounced it along the Trail at the places where she was staying for more than a day. First things first, she dug into the toiletries that included everything a girl might want like soap, conditioner, lotion, a razor, dental floss, and tweezers.

Moments later, Alex was in pure bliss as the hot water from

the showerhead poured down on the crown of her head. She scrubbed away all of the dirt and grime, washed her hair twice, shaved, and soaked up every bit of the soap and water she could. After the shower, she padded around the room naked and utterly comfortable. Since her cell phone was plugged into the wall outlet, she quickly connected to the hotel's Wi-Fi and started listening to the Acoustic Covers playlist on Spotify. The sound of music immediately filled the room, a sound her ears weren't accustomed to on the Trail. Music always had a way of lightening her mood. She looked at her five-foot-seven-inch reflection in the mirror and noticed she had lost more weight. Without a scale in the room she wasn't sure, but by the looks of it, she was nearing her high school weight of 135 pounds—a number she hadn't seen in she couldn't remember how long. Her body was changing, that was for sure. Her legs were more muscular, her shoulders and neck stronger. Her dark wavy hair fell just at her shoulders. Before she left, she'd cut off nearly ten inches to her sister's dismay, knowing she'd want less hair to manage while hiking. The style had grown on her. It was layered and soft and easy to manage. Since losing so much weight, her dark brown eyes looked larger and rounder than she was accustomed to and her cleft chin was a lot more pronounced than before. The transformation didn't bother her. She liked the way she looked. It was as if she finally felt completely comfortable in her own skin.

After cleaning herself down to filing her fingernails, she threw on a pair of shorts and a tank top that she kept in her bounce box so she had something to wear while her hiking clothes were in the laundry. She had to pull the drawstring to her shorts tight just to keep them on her hips.

She tore open the box from Marcie and Emma, finding a note at the top.

Dear Alex:

Here are a few little gifts to make you smile and maybe a little more.

Hugs and love, M and E.

Alex pulled out a few scraps of newspaper and found three things: a small bottle of Jack Daniels Honey, her favorite; a small LELO vibrator; and a package of home-baked chocolate-chip-and-walnut cookies. She laughed. Only her best friends would send her these three perfectly random and perfect gifts. She thought about which to enjoy first, and opted for stuffing a soft and perfect cookie into her mouth.

After inhaling three cookies, she forced herself to zip the bag closed before she devoured the entire batch. She left the other gifts for later, grabbed her debit card, and headed for the taproom for that cheeseburger. The third box from her sister remained unopened. She'd open that later when she returned.

The burger might well have been the best burger of her life. It was so good she ordered a second burger platter and a second Guinness, to the shock of the waitress. The taproom was pretty empty since it was in between lunch and dinner but Alex couldn't care less. She checked her phone, and got caught up on the sixty-two text messages from her sister, her mom, Marcie, and Emma. Usually she avoided Facebook, but today she caught up on everyone's lives, and even made a selfie post with the burger and beers.

She texted Marcie and Emma thanking them for the gifts.

Thank you for the box of goodies!

Emma responded: *Our PLEASURE.*

Marcie added a little cigarette pack emoji from her new collection of lesbian emojis that made Alex laugh out loud in the empty dining room.

After stuffing herself, she decided to stroll around town on the hunt for ice cream.

These were the moments when she missed the company of her closest friends on the Trail. For some reason being alone in the woods never made her feel lonely at all but when she was back in civilization with people all around, she became acutely aware that she was alone and most everyone else wasn't. She stopped for her favorite black raspberry ice cream and continued strolling down

Main Street. Her pace slowed in front a quaint gift shop as she looked at a rack of artistic greeting cards. "Light the World Aflame" caught her eye. She finished her cone and entered the eclectic shop. After browsing for a few minutes, she decided on a cute wallet made from recycled plastic bags for her sister and lavender hand lotion for her mom. She'd send them out at the post office before she headed back out on the Trail in a few days.

Alex stopped at an art gallery and looked at the beautiful watercolor paintings and serene photographs. She felt the familiar tightness in her chest. Art. It was always something she shared with Cate. Before Cate, she never paid much attention to it, but Cate had taught her to appreciate art and the artists who created it. She was with Cate the first time she purchased a large piece of art from a reputable gallery. They were together in North Adams for a weekend getaway because Cate wanted to visit the Massachusetts Museum of Contemporary Art or MoCA. It was there that Alex watched Cate talk to another artist about their craft. Their language was all their own and Alex loved the way Cate lit up when she talked about making art. It was there that they got high in the bedroom of the bed and breakfast, blowing smoke out the small bathroom window, and for the first time in her life, Alex felt the world spin off its axis because she finally found someone who made her feel renewed, complete, and utterly alive in each moment. They didn't even kiss that weekend. They just spent the entire weekend together, laughing and enjoying life in each sprawling moment as if no one else existed outside the realm of the world they created. It was magical and an experience Alex never felt with another person in her life.

Alex stepped out of the gallery, unable to continue looking at art. The memories were too vivid. Yet another thing she used to do that was ruined after Cate. Come to think of it, most everything reminded her of Cate but she hadn't quite learned how to block out the entire world.

Early evening enveloped everything in a hazy, orange, sunlit soft focus, and she decided to return to the room for a long and leisurely night alone in bed. As she walked down the street, she became aware of her feet touching the pavement. Pavement could be so unforgiving compared to the leaves and dirt of the Trail. She felt the reverberation of each step in her calves. Main Street looked so warm and inviting, a quintessential New England town on a beautiful summer evening. It reminded her of home and she felt that familiar tug of homesickness once again. This was the longest she had ever been away from her home and her family and at times the pull toward home was almost unbearable. The crickets began their tune-up for the evening and even the traffic of the oncoming cars seemed to move slower, more leisurely. These were the moments Alex felt now, noticed now, more than she ever did before. Since hiking, her awareness of moments shifted and became so much clearer. Before hiking, she spent most of her time rushing from one place to another barely noticing much of anything outside the confines of her home or job or family. These many days alone already taught her to breathe deeply, to savor every moment, to allow the loneliness to pass through her rather than remaining cooped up inside of her. She was reminded of a quote she saw once: "The worst feeling isn't being lonely but being forgotten by someone you can't forget." She wondered if Cate forgot her already. She wondered if Cate missed her or thought about her while she as at her artist residency in Provincetown. She pushed the thoughts aside. Suddenly she was so incredibly tired.

Once snug in bed, she decided to call her sister.

Sara picked up on the first ring.

"Hey, sis."

"Hey, you! Are you clean, well fed, and all snuggled up in bed?"

Alex laughed. Her sister knew her too well. "Yep."

"Well? Did you open the box?"

"Oh, no! I decided to wait until later. Why?"

"You received a letter from work. I didn't open it, but it can't be good," Sara said, the worry evident in her voice.

"Hang on." Alex put her cell on speaker and dropped it on the bed. She reluctantly climbed from the bed and grabbed the box off the floor. She sifted through clothes, food supplies, and letters and found the one her sister referred to. She tore open the envelope and read the short, typewritten memo silently.

"Well? What does it say? Alex?"

"It says they don't need me to come back at all this school year. They've found a permanent replacement. They couldn't afford to keep a substitute on for the first three months of the school year for me to finish my hike. So, it looks like I'm now out of a job on top of everything else."

"I knew they weren't going to honor your leave of absence. What are you going to do?"

Alex didn't even hesitate in her response. "Keep hiking."

"Alex, you can't be serious. You need to come home and talk to them. I bet if you come home now they'll give you your job back. I know you want to hike the whole Trail but you need a job. You have a mortgage. Bills to pay. Remember real life?"

"I can't stop hiking now."

"Alex, get real. It's a hike. You have your entire life to think about here."

"I am getting real. I'm getting more real on this hike than I have my whole life. You know, I don't think I ever knew myself. Really knew myself. If I walk away from the Trail now, I will regret it for the rest of my life and as it is, I am piling up more regrets lately than I ever wanted to have. So no, I won't go back to work. Screw them. I'll find another job when I get back. I have a pretty decent savings that will get me through the next few months. I've always been so damned responsible. I'll figure something out, but not until I finish this hike."

"I'm not sure if I think you're crazy brave or just plain crazy. I love you and I'm worried about you. Mom is going to have a coronary over this. As it is, she wanted to drive down tonight to see you. She saw your selfie picture on Facebook and said you are skin and bones. I had to bribe her to keep her promise and stay out of your hair."

"Don't tell her. The less she knows the better anyway. I've started writing again. Maybe I'll write a book about my experience," said Alex, a wry, sarcastic tone in her voice.

"That's great, babe. But writing a book isn't going to put food on the table or pay your electric bill."

"You're such a downer. I've got to go. I'll call you tomorrow. Love you and thanks for all the goodies." Alex tried not to let the worry creep into her voice.

"I love you too. Get some rest."

After Alex hung up with her sister, she looked through the remaining mail and checked out the uninspiring but necessary dehydrated food her sister packed for her. She almost forgot about the two other gifts her best friends had given her. Those made her smile immediately. She cracked open the little bottle of Jack Daniels Honey and poured it over ice. This was usually her favorite cold-weather drink, but it felt just as smooth going down in the middle of the summer and it reminded her even more of home.

She held the small purple vibrator in her hand and thought about whether or not to even use it. Her sexual appetites had been nonexistent since Cate but tonight in this beautiful, romantic hotel room, all she wanted to do was forget about the fact she was alone for a while. The alcohol warmed her from the inside, helping her relax even more. She stripped off her clothes and lay down on the bed in the darkness listening to soft music surround her. The light from the vibrator partially illuminated the room and reminded Alex of the first night she and Cate made love during a snowstorm when the power had gone out and all they had were candles and a kerosene lantern casting a soft, warm glow around Cate's loft. She closed her eyes and willed herself back to that time and place as the vibrator made her body feel things she had last felt with Cate. Her own body surprised her by climaxing over and over again, each with mounting intensity, for well over an hour. Truthfully, she could have continued long into the night but she was suddenly bored and tired with the one-sided lovemaking. So, she pulled the pristine white sheet over her body and thought about getting back out on the Trail. Her spacious suite seemed cramped and stale and she longed once more for the open air and the woods all around her.

CHAPTER 8

August 14, 2014 11:25 p.m.
Salisbury, Connecticut

*D*ear Cate:
      I'm taking a break from the Trail for a few days to rest my legs. I'm in this incredibly beautiful suite in Salisbury, Connecticut that reminds me of the place we stayed at in North Adams. You'd love it here. There are these terrific art galleries and shops. I saw a painting today that reminded me of the first painting I bought when we were together. That painting still hangs over my bed at home. Home. I can't bear it anymore. Too many memories of you, of us, in it. I had to get away from there. I needed fresh air and new memories that had nothing to do with us. I finally understand your need to keep moving from place to place. I never did before. Now I appreciate what you meant by going wherever the wind blows.

    It's late, and I should be sleeping but I can't. I'm not used to sleeping inside anymore. It feels stuffy in here with the air conditioning on. I officially lost my job today, and I should be thinking about that, but as I tossed and turned in bed, my thoughts kept turning back to you. Once, I even reached over and felt like you were there next to me. Thinking of you in the late-night hours, when I imagine your face or your smile, usually comforts me and helps me to relax. Alone late at night, I can be free with you in my imagination. I don't have to stop myself. I don't question anything. I just think of you, and I become peaceful, serene, and always very happy.

Instead of becoming relaxed at the thought of you, the opposite happened. I woke up completely. I didn't feel peace. I felt alive and awake and wanting so much to be nearer to you. The need inside me was so overwhelming I started a text message to tell you where I was in the vague hope you would come find me, and everything would be okay. But then, I realized that would be a mistake because you made it clear that you could not see a future with us, so I deleted the text and tried to go back to sleep. When that didn't happen, I got up and decided to write to you instead.

I saw a card in a store that read, "Light the World Aflame." You do light my world aflame. You heat me up in my core, in my soul, and I struggle to find solid ground. I struggle to cool off, and I struggle to keep myself together.

Ugh. I just read that back, and it sounds so dramatic. Sometimes I hate that my thoughts of you are so dramatic. They are true, but I over-analyze everything—even how I describe my world to you. Which is funny actually since I doubt you'll ever read these words anyway.

I don't know why I keep thinking about this, but I can't let go of the time you sent me a Facebook post on the anniversary of my dad's death. At the time, I was angry with you. I wondered if our friendship meant so little to you that you actually thought a Facebook post was enough to help me mourn the death of my father. Maybe there will come a time when you realize that people need you as much as you need them, that running away isn't an answer. I know you are an artist and as such, you'll always be pretty self-absorbed. What? You are. It's the only quality about you that I dislike. You think the world revolves around you. I know you will grow up and realize that is not true. I long for the day *when I can home to your sweet face. No matter where I am, yours are the arms I long for.*

Always,

Alex

CHAPTER 9

CATE

August 2014
Provincetown, Massachusetts

A week into her residency in Provincetown, and now nearly four months after running away from Alex and everything she was building in Stockbridge, Cate lounged in a hammock on the porch of her dune shack with one golden tanned leg dangling over the side as she ate a snickerdoodle cookie, and stared up at the white, powder-puff cumulus clouds. She wondered what clouds must actually feel like to touch. Were they like cotton candy, melting the moment the heat from her skin touched them? Did they feel like cotton balls? She was mostly trying to figure out if she could see beyond them, behind them to the blue and lighter blue hues, fascinated with how the colors changed as the light shifted from moment to moment. Something was mesmerizing about the light here in Provincetown. She read about it before, and it was one of the primary reasons she wanted to stay. Since the arrival of a railroad in Provincetown in 1873 that made it accessible to visit, painters stayed in boarding houses for as little as fifty dollars a year to study the light. She finally understood why. The railroad was long since gone, but the artists kept coming back year after year, turning it into one of the most famous artists' colonies in the country.

Earlier in the morning, a group of six aspiring young artists came by as part of the National Seashore's Interpretive Program. She didn't mind the visitors touring the shack and asking her questions about her art, especially since they'd also delivered the snickerdoodle cookies, root beer, and ice. She didn't ask for cookies and root beer, but the program visitors delivered them just the same as a thank-you and to help her stay energized to keep painting. The poor young artists didn't know that she had little actual art to show for her residency thus far. But, she wasn't one to turn down cookies or root beer or ice for that matter.

And so, she lay there in the hammock making shapes out of the clouds feeling like a total and utter fraud. Artists tried for years to land these residencies, yet all she did with her time was think about Alex and waste away whole days one after the other. The thought occurred to her that she should probably pack up and leave to allow a real artist the chance to do something productive with the remaining time.

"Hello? Is anybody home?" a woman's voice rang out from behind the dune shack.

Cate perked up in her hammock. "Mama?" Cate's voice rose in surprised recognition. She wasn't expecting any visitors during her stay, but it was just like her mother to turn up unannounced at exactly the moment when she needed her most.

"Hey, Sweet Pea!" Her mother's voice was louder as she moved to the side of the shack. Sandra Conrad carried a blue bucket sloshing with water, a twelve-pack of Red Stripe Jamaican beer, and a worn and sun-bleached backpack. At fifty-eight years old, Cate's mother looked incredible. She was tall and athletic and in fantastic shape. Cate got her blond curls and coloring from her mom, but her blue eyes were all her father's.

Cate jumped out of the hammock and ran to her mother. She

hugged her so tightly she heard her mother wheeze as she squeezed the air from her lungs. Cate looked down into the bucket and jumped at the two live lobsters splashing around.

"I brought dinner," her mom said, smiling broadly. It was so typical for her mother to show up unannounced with lobsters—so typical, and so utterly perfect.

"Mom, what are you doing here and how did you find me?" Cate shaded the sun from her eyes with one hand.

"I'm here to visit my daughter. And you weren't difficult to find. I just asked around town. They pointed me in the direction of Art's Dune Tours. You didn't sound like yourself when we talked a couple of weeks ago. Am I wrong, or am I right?"

"You're right, of course. I'm so happy you're here. Where's Dad?"

"Oh, he's staying in town looking at what else? Sailboats. He says hello, but he knew I wanted some alone time with my little girl."

"Mama, I'm not a little girl. I'm thirty-one years old." Cate laughed.

"I don't care how old you are. You'll always be my little girl."

"How do you always know when I need you most?" Cate asked, hugging her mother again.

"A mother always knows, Sweet Pea. Now show me around this beautiful abode."

Cate gave her mother the five-cent tour that lasted all of a minute. Her mother unrolled her own sleeping bag next to Cate's and put her paintbrushes in a mason jar next to Cate's.

After they had safely ensconced the lobsters in the shade and the beer in the newly delivered ice, they went down to the beach for a long, leisurely swim. Afterward, mother and daughter swung in the hammock opposite one another soaking in the late after-noon sun and sipping beer from the bottle.

"I feel like we're in the middle of a Corona commercial, except with Red Stripe," remarked Cate as they lazily swayed back and forth.

"Mmm hmm. That's the best way to live." After a few moments, her mother continued. "So, judging from the blank canvases inside, you're not finding this place very inspiring?"

"Way to jump right into the heavy stuff," Cate said, bristling a little. "Of course, this place is inspiring. I don't know. I can't focus. I don't have a clear thought. And just when I think I've got it together enough to start a painting, the light is gone, and I'm pacing around the inside of that shack for the rest of the night."

"You've always been a pacer. Whenever you had something on your mind you paced. I remember when you were seven you paced back and forth inside the cabin for two full nights after your stuffed bear fell overboard." Her mother chuckled at the memory. "Even Magellan was annoyed with you. What's going on in that beautiful mind of yours?"

Cate hesitated. She hadn't told her parents about Alex yet. It's not that she thought they would care about her being with another woman. She'd been with other women in the past, and they knew about them all. She hadn't been able to tell them because telling them would make it all too real, and reality was exactly what she had been escaping from.

"You've gone and fallen in love, haven't you?" Cate's mother asked gently. Seagulls glided over their heads, casting fleeting V-shaped shadows across the sand. The sun had begun its slow descent. The air took on a golden, shimmering hue, making both Cate and her mother's blond hair glisten even more than normal. The two looked so alike in the hammock they seemed almost otherworldly atop the remote dunes, as if suspended by nothing but clouds.

Cate couldn't respond, but a few stray tears escaped and slowly glided down her cheeks.

"What's her name?" Her mother gently tried to coax the story from Cate.

"Alex. Alex McKenzie. She's an English teacher at Burr. That's how we met."

"Well, that was eight months ago, and you're still this shaken up?"

Cate didn't respond. She turned her head toward the golden horizon instead.

"Oh, honey. Love is a beautiful, miraculous gift. Alex must be a very special person for you to feel the way you do. What are you so afraid of?" Her mother leaned forward in the hammock and softly held Cate's feet.

"She is special, really special. But I messed it up, Mama."

"Everything can be fixed."

"Not this time. I broke her heart. I told her I didn't love her, and then I watched as her heart broke right there in front of me. The worst part was, I lied."

"Well then, why did you tell her you didn't love her?" her mother asked.

"Because I was afraid. She made me feel things. She made me question my freedom or my wanting freedom. Mama, she's so settled, so steady. It scared me. What if she wanted to stay in Stockbridge for the rest of our lives? I couldn't bear it, being stuck like that, especially landlocked." Cate's voice rose an octave at the mere thought of it.

"You know, when I met your father, it felt as though I'd finally come home. It never mattered where we lived or where our little sailboat floated to, so long as I was with him—and you when you came along—I was home. Your father and I found a way to exert our freedom without losing one another. I remember when we lived in Vermont and your father was working that awful nine-to-five job in the accounting firm. He was so miserable, but he had been brought up to sacrifice his dreams to provide for his family. I couldn't stand the feeling that we were tied down to a house and a mortgage, and I couldn't stand the look on your father's face when he returned from work exhausted each night. I was watching him slowly die. I was watching us slowly die all while we were doing what everyone else did. The best decision we ever made was selling the house and buying that boat. Falling in love with someone doesn't mean you will lose your freedom, it means you've finally found it because, for all the wandering, you'll never do it alone."

Her mother was right, of course. Maybe it was "only-child syndrome," but Cate had valued her independence so much it had cost her the love of her life. "Well, it's too late now. I doubt she'll ever speak to me again. I mean, why would she?"

"If she loves you the way you love her, of course, she will speak to you again. The universe has a funny way of working things out. You just have to find a way to open yourself up again. Let it go, sweetheart, and stop blaming yourself. Just try to be present in each beautiful moment, and allow yourself to feel again. Once you start to feel, you'll start making art and once you start making art, you'll be right as rain."

"Oh, Mama. I've missed you so much."

"I missed you too, Sweet Pea. Now let's go cook some lobsters!"

CHAPTER 10

August 22, 2014 8:05 p.m.
Provincetown, Massachusetts

*D*ear Alex:

My mother just left after surprising me in Provincetown. We didn't party or go into town. We walked the beach, swam, and laughed a lot. We found an old lobster pot and set it. We ate fresh lobster every night. We even went clamming at low tide using our feet to dig up the biggest quahog clams I've ever seen. My mom has this incredible way of making every moment real and true and filled with love. I learned how to paint watching both my parents. Painting is something my mother does like breathing. It's so effortless for her. She said she never experienced an artistic block in her life. I apparently didn't get that gene. My mother gently guided me toward the blank canvas and somehow got me painting again. I'm not sure how she did it. It's the first time I've felt immersed in my art in a long time. It felt good. My mother always knows how to soothe me.

It's hard for me to imagine you here with me. I only seem to see you in Stockbridge, never anywhere else. I'm not even sure if you feel at home at the beach the way I do. There is so much I still don't know about you. Do you love the ocean? Do you love the way the sand warms in the early morning sun and reflects back the light from above? I wish I could taste the ocean on your lips as I kiss you here. I wish I could lick the white salt from your skin and tell you with my mouth how much I have missed you. Instead, all I can do is paint and dream because I screwed it up. I screwed us up.

The sun just set. Everything is in shadows. A red fox just appeared in front of my window and looked up at me. I'm playing music on a little battery radio, and I think he likes it. It's instrumental guitar and reminds me of the time we went to the bar and heard that flamenco guitarist play. Your hand was on my leg, and I felt dizzy that night. I would have taken you in the bathroom if you let me but you were too shy and your shyness made me want you more. We barely made it back to your house before I tore your clothes off. I needed to feel every inch of your body, to smell your skin and hear you call out my name. No one feels like you do. No one makes me feel the way you do. Oh, Alex, I'm so sorry. Please forgive me. Please help me find my way back to you.

Love,

Cate

CHAPTER 11

CATE

January 2014
Stockbridge, Massachusetts

On a cold winter January afternoon seven months earlier, Cate stood outside Alex's classroom as the last students straggled out. She peeked her head in and watched Alex walk up and down the aisles, picking up papers or straightening out desks. Cate noticed the way Alex moved and felt the butterflies kick in her stomach. She hardly knew this woman, yet every fiber of her being gently pulled her toward Alex. It was undeniable.

Cate stepped into the room and closed the door, startling Alex. "Hi."

"Hi," Alex replied curtly.

After a few awkward and silent moments, Cate took a few more steps toward her. She bucked up and spoke. "Listen I just wanted to apologize for the other night. I don't know what came over me."

"You couldn't get out of there fast enough from the looks of it," said Alex, continuing to tidy the classroom.

Cate shifted her weight from foot to foot. These were uncharted waters for her.

"I like you, and I want to get to know you better," said Cate.

"You have a funny way of showing it. I mean, you just up and walked out. Who does that?"

"I know. I got nervous. I'm not good at sharing feelings."

Alex stopped what she was doing and walked up so close Cate could smell her perfume. Cate noticed the way Alex's hair was tucked behind one ear, exposing her long neck. She resisted the urge to lean in and kiss Alex there in the warm spot beneath her ear.

"Cate, why are you here?" Alex asked, her voice barely above a whisper. Alex leaned in closer. They were standing as close as two people could without touching. Cate felt Alex's breath move her hair. The air buzzed between them with electricity as if a current ran from Cate to Alex and back again. Cate leaned forward to kiss Alex, but Alex abruptly pulled away and broke the connection between them.

"Not here," Alex said. "And how do I know you won't run the next time?"

Cate smiled. "Does that mean there will be a next time?" she asked, hopeful.

"Maybe," Alex said, hedging.

Cate seized the opportunity. "Why don't you come with me on a little weekend road trip? I'm going to North Adams to check out the Massachusetts Museum of Modern Art. I already have a room booked at a cute bed and breakfast."

Cate could see the hesitation pass over Alex's face, but it finally gave way to a slight smile. "Sure. I guess I could get away for the weekend."

"Great! I'll pick you up tomorrow morning around ten o'clock. It should take us about an hour to get there, which gives us plenty of time to visit the museum." Cate was genuinely excited to go away with Alex but made a silent promise to herself not to push things too quickly, mostly for her own sake rather than Alex's. She was already having a hard time holding back from kissing Alex, but she vowed not to go beyond that for now. She was excited but scared, and she was dead set on not screwing things up again between them.

~

Cate's fingers drummed the steering wheel of her old beat-up Subaru Outback as she waited in front of Alex's house on an extremely dry and cold January morning. She was nervous; there was no denying that. The thought of spending two uninterrupted days with Alex made her stomach flip. Alex finally emerged from her house carrying an overnight bag.

"Hi," said Alex as she loaded her bag into the back seat and settled herself, loosening her knitted scarf and unzipping her parka. "It's freezing out today."

"It is. No snow in the forecast but we'll be lucky if the temps rise out of the teens." Cate motioned to the center console. "There's a cup of coffee for you. Wasn't sure how you took it, so it's black, but there are cream and sugar in the bag."

"Perfect. Thank you! I drink it black anyway." Alex wrapped her hands around the hot coffee as the steam encircled her face. Cate hit the accelerator.

They drove in companionable silence for a few minutes, Alex sipping her coffee. Cate turned on the radio. "What kind of music do you like?" she asked.

"Anything except heavy metal, bluegrass, or country," Alex responded. "I love classical music, especially on Sunday mornings and my favorite instrument is the guitar. I took lessons for a while but the teacher told me I couldn't sing so I stopped. I remember being so embarrassed."

"How old were you?" Cate asked, incredulous.

"I was about fourteen years old. I never picked up the guitar again. I think that's when I subconsciously decided to become a teacher. Sometimes teachers don't realize how much power and influence they have over kids. And she was one awful teacher."

Cate settled on her favorite, the Coffeehouse, an acoustic folk station on Sirius XM. For the next hour, their conversation remained light. Nothing too intensely personal was shared, but Cate learned a lot about Alex. Alex told her about her sister Sara, and it seemed as though the two sisters had an incredibly tight bond. It never fazed Cate that she was an only child until she hit her twenties. Then she longed for a sister, a best friend, someone who shared her unique adolescence.

Judging from the way Alex peppered Cate with questions about living aboard a sailboat, she was beyond intrigued by Cate's childhood. Questions like: "How did you shower?" "Were you ever scared you'd sink?" "Did your parents have any privacy? I mean what if they wanted to have sex or something?" The barrage of questions went on and on. Cate had dozens of memories in the archives to pull from. At one point Alex interrupted Cate's story about a hurricane and a close call when they were in the Florida Keys and asked a seemingly simple question: "Wait, so how many places *have* you been?"

"Hmm. Let me think. These might not be in order but let me try. The Florida Keys, New Orleans, Cancun, the Bahamas, the Cayman Islands, Jamaica, the Dominican Republic, the Virgin Islands, Aruba, Curacao, a bunch of port cities in Spain, Portugal, Casablanca, Monaco, all around Italy, and eastern Greece. We steered completely clear of anything from Cape Verde south for fear of pirates and never had any issues in that regard, thank God."

Alex was silent.

"I know, it's a lot of places, right? Some of them I don't even remember that well. And that doesn't include most of the East Coast."

"Well let's compare your travels to mine. I've been to Florida,

Washington DC, the Jersey shore, parts of Connecticut and Rhode Island, and Bermuda for a long weekend trip. Once we took a trip to Vermont and Maine. I've been on an airplane twice my entire life: once to Disney World and once to Bermuda. It's like you were just casually reading from a world map as though it were no big deal. It's literally unimaginable to me," Alex said wistfully.

"Well it wasn't always sunshine and roses you know," Cate said as she adjusted her rearview mirror. "Sometimes I wished I had a normal life and normal parents. I never had a birthday party like every other kid. My birthdays were spent in unfamiliar places with a bunch of local kids I most likely never saw before or would never see again."

Cate was silent for a moment as she sipped her coffee and returned it to the cup holder. "I never made any close friends because we moved around so much. We never had a Christmas tree. Sometimes the boat felt so cramped, and I envied the kids on shore who ran around from place to place with freedom. I rarely understood the language except for little bits and pieces I could pick up. Don't get me wrong, I wouldn't trade it for anything, but it wasn't the fairy tale life you might think it was." Cate stole a glance at Alex, who was openly gazing at her, so much so it made Cate suddenly self-conscious and shy.

"Maybe not a fairy tale, but pretty damned exciting," said Alex.

Three hours later, they stood on the third floor of the Sol LeWitt exhibition, A Wall Drawing Retrospective, comprised of 105 of LeWitt's large-scale wall drawings. The exhibit was spectacular. The interior walls were specially built to the artist's specifications and occupied three stories of the historic mill building in the heart of MASS MoCA's campus.

"Wow," breathed Cate, looking at the colorful wall drawing of whirls and twirls. "His ideas are so consistent, and he's so disciplined. I could never do that. It's amazing." She and Alex stood side by side, allowing the art to surround them both. "It's as if he wanted you to stop and be immersed in all the color. It's so vibrant and optimistic.

Another middle-aged female patron stood nearby and overheard Cate's comments. "Sorry, I didn't mean to eavesdrop," she said. "But I overheard your conversation. You must be an artist too."

"I am," replied Cate.

"I tend to gravitate toward realism, but this is just marvelous. And I have to say I feel the same way. I mean LeWitt was pivotal in the creation of the new radical aesthetic of the sixties, but I just find it so remarkable that he had no interest in inherent narrative or descriptive imagery."

Cate loved visiting galleries and looking at art, and she loved talking about it too. Her insides lit up at the intense creativity of others, and this Sol LeWitt exhibition was not a disappointment. "I heard some people compare his work to street art, but this is so not street art. It's not mainstream art in that way. You can tell he clearly meant for his art to be experienced indoors in a place like this," Cate continued, marveling at the large geometric blocks of color all around.

"It's such a shame he didn't live long enough to see this exhibit," the female patron said. "Anyway, enjoy your visit."

"Sure thing, take care," said Cate politely as the woman walked away.

Suddenly, Alex took Cate's hand in hers and looked at her with a mildly surprised expression. Cate's fingers tightened around Alex's as if to tell her she liked the contact and wanted it to continue.

"It's so interesting watching you talk about art. It's as if you become alive with it. I mean you are the most alive person I've ever been around, but watching you in here, it's like you go to a whole other level of aliveness if that makes any sense. Cate, you're really so beautiful."

Cate felt a blush coming on. She wanted so badly to kiss Alex right there in the middle of the Sol LeWitt exhibit, but she didn't dare a repeat of Alex pulling away. Instead, she touched Alex's cheek with her fingertips and said ever so quietly, "You're beautiful too."

The two stood in the middle of the room, surrounded by all the geometric, colorful art in their own world until Cate broke the spell. "Let's get a drink."

"That sounds great," replied Alex as they walked through the exhibit hand in hand.

Later that evening after drinks, dinner, and a short, near-frozen stroll through town, Cate and Alex lay sprawled on a high four-poster queen-size bed, both fully clothed, staring at the ceiling in a state of utter relaxation. Cate had brought a couple of joints with her and was thrilled when Alex welcomed the idea of smoking them together. Their room at the Porches Inn was cozy and comfortable as the winter wind howled outside. After they smoked the joints, careful to blow the smoke out the small bathroom window, they listened to a Spotify playlist entitled Fleet Foxes, The Weepies, Good Stuff, letting the current song "Down in the Valley" from The Head and the Heart fill the room. The decorative plates affixed to the wall fascinated Cate.

"I just don't understand how anyone could eat with the plates like that," she said. "The food would just slide right off."

Alex laughed at Cate's marijuana musings, and Cate rolled over to face her, drawn to the sound of her laughter.

"Do that again," she said.

"Do what?" asked Alex.

"Laugh."

"I can't just laugh on cue. I'm not a trained seal," quipped Alex.

"First of all, I wasn't aware trained seals were known for laughing on cue." Cate leaned up on her elbow. "Second, it's such a pretty sound. Has anyone ever told you what a pretty laugh you have? Pretty. So pretty." A warm glow of contentment filled Cate's insides.

"Oh, I love this song," said Alex, her hands above her head. "Falling Slowly" played from the movie *Once*. Cate just stared at Alex, listening to the words of the song as if they were written for the two of them at that exact moment.

"Were you ever in love?" asked Cate, openly staring at Alex's mouth, her neck, her breasts.

Alex continued to stare at the ceiling. "That's hard to say. I guess I was in love maybe twice, but they were different each time, and I think it was more about growing up and learning what I wanted and didn't want from someone, rather than falling head over heels in love. Does that make sense?"

"Sort of," Cate said, trying to understand and trying to focus herself on Alex's words and not her lips.

"How about you?" Alex tilted her head to one side. "Anyone special in your past?"

Cate tried to figure out how to explain as she picked at some lint on Alex's sleeve. "There was someone once a long time ago. We were really young. It was a doomed summer romance. I always wanted something long-term and stable, someone to come home to, but I never had a home long enough in one place." Cate surprised herself with how much she had just admitted to Alex. For a moment, it seemed as though Alex had slept through her entire explanation, but then Alex shifted and Cate realized she heard every word.

Alex turned and faced Cate, looking at her with such intent, Cate sighed.

"I want to kiss you," Cate said matter-of-factly, as she ran her fingertips down Alex's arm and side.

"I know you do. You've been staring at my lips for like an hour," Alex said playfully.

"I want to make love to you," Cate continued, her fingers sliding down Alex's hip to her leg and knee.

"You barely know me!" Alex gave her a look of pretend shock as she leaned in closer.

"That's not true," said Cate. "I know a great deal about you. You can't pretend you don't feel this chemistry between us."

"Of course, I feel the chemistry between us." Alex ran her thumb over Cate's full lips and hovered for a moment just inches from her face. The energy between them smoldered, but Alex pulled back first. "Please let's not rush this. Let's just be in the moment like this a little while longer. Everything will change after we do all of that, but right now we are in such a perfect place I don't want to mess with it. Okay?"

"Okay," Cate said hesitantly, removing her hand from Alex's leg. She was high but not so high that she didn't let those words sink in. Everything would change after they made love. This was not going to be a one-night stand or a casual fling. She knew it and realized Alex did too. Cate just didn't realize the degree of those changes until many months later.

CHAPTER 12

ALEX

August 2014
Appalachian Trail, Connecticut

*A*lex expertly shoved aside memories of winter with Cate that past January as she just as expertly hoisted her full pack onto her back in one smooth motion and checked around the room at the White Hart Inn in Salisbury for the last time. Three days of rest and relaxation had passed quickly. Her gifts home were in the mail. Her bills were paid for another month. Her bounce box was sent on ahead to her next two-night stop in Warwick, New York, about twelve days and 127.5 miles away. She planned to average about ten miles per day, which seemed a bit light for a seasoned hiker like her but she knew she had hot weather and a lot of elevation with Bear Mountain to deal with. She wore clean clothes and had fresh batteries and plenty of food. She was fully charged for the road ahead. She'd make at least one food-resupply stop along the way but she wouldn't leave the Trail unless she had to. The moments when she left town again for the Trail always gave her butterflies. It's as if she was re-stripping away all the normalcy and noise of civilization. As she stepped back out into the great unknown, the Trail had become more and more her home.

She walked back down Main Street and tried to take a mental picture of the town that she could store away in her memory. It was a place Cate would have loved. Maybe one day they would come back here together.

Most people imagined the Appalachian Trail as this scenic gravel road with stunning vistas at every turn. But in reality, much of the Trail was rather confining, especially in the summer when the trees formed a dense canopy of leaves. At times the Trail felt much like a green tunnel: rocky, jagged, and steep. The section Alex hiked now was all of those things in one. She hiked up just to hike down again, with little vantage points from one mile to the next. She hiked on in the direction of Bear Mountain, a spot she had deemed her personal mission to reach. That was where her father took her and Sara camping so many years ago. That was the place she first fell in love with the woods and the way the earth smelled early in the morning. She remembered lying on her back with her head in the crook of her father's arm and Sara on the other side. They stayed like that for hours, staring up at the night sky, counting shooting stars. Her father told stories of fantastic sea creatures and pirate ships that he made up out of thin air. They ate s'mores for dinner and scraped their knees on rock scrambles like the Lemon Squeeze. She felt safe and alive there with her father and sister. She never imagined that a year later, her mother would be handed a folded American flag at her father's funeral.

She had many miles to walk before she reached Bear Mountain, but it was her touchstone. Every mile was one mile closer to those special memories with her father. On this day, the miles wore on and she found herself guzzling through twice the water she normally did. Even though the canopy kept the sun off her, it was still and humid, and she figured the temperatures were somewhere in the upper eighties. She crossed the Housatonic River and passed Falls Village without stopping. At the hydroelectric plant, she saw signs for a cold shower. Even though she'd just left town that morning, the joy of cold, clean water was too much to pass up. She stopped for lunch that included a turkey sandwich, apple, and a Gatorade she'd bought in town that morning. After lunch she rinsed off in her shorts and tank top. She looked up at the bright blue sky as the ice-cold water poured down her face. She soaked in the refreshing water and the simple beauty of the moment she found herself in. Life was made up of these small, seemingly insignificant moments when she felt truly alive and at peace with the world around her. She lounged in the shade for longer than she should have before lacing up her boots once again to knock out the remaining few miles of hiking for the day.

After hiking a hair over eleven miles, she finally stopped to make camp at the Sharon Mountain campsite just after six o'clock in the evening. There was no lean-to shelter, but there was a large area for tents. Several other northbound thru-hikers were already settling in for the night. Since she had a hammock and not a tent, she found a level spot at the tree line and set up her camp. Although she stayed in shelters most of the time, she loved her Eno Junglenest hammock. It was super light and took all of about two minutes tops to set up. Because she knew the weather forecast was clear and warm for the night, she didn't bother setting up a rainfly or even inflating her mattress pad. She unrolled her sleeping bag inside the hammock and made sure the bug net line above her head was high enough to provide her plenty of headroom once inside the hammock. Her food would be hung far away as usual and the rest of her gear hung from a carabiner below her hammock, just off the ground. After her camp was set up, she strolled over to the viewpoint to check out the area around the mountain. The vista was magnificent, highlighted by several hang gliders swirling above her head. She shaded her eyes with her hands to get a better look at the gliders moving effortlessly back and forth. She had read in her trail guidebook that this view looked out over Lime Rock Park, where the late Paul Newman and other celebrities sped their cars around the classic 1.53-mile racecourse. There were no races today, just the gliders skimming across the sky.

"Wow. They're amazing aren't they?" A man's voice surprised her from behind.

"Yeah, they sure are," responded Alex.

"Sorry, I didn't mean to startle you. I'm MacGyver. I just set up camp myself."

"I'm Alex." She sized up the young man quickly and found him friendly and harmless. By the length of his beard, the state of his hiking boots, and the rips in his T-shirt, she could tell he was a Northbounder who'd been on the Trail for quite a while.

"Wait, what's your Trail name?"

Asking someone's Trail name was a surefire conversation starter and also a great Trail tradition, but hiking solo southbound left few opportunities to spend quality time with other hikers who could help name her. Trail names often preceded the hikers in long-distance hiking circles. The name typically matched the hiker's personality as well as their exploits and experiences on the Trail. Practically speaking, the names were useful since there were a lot of Shawns and Daves and Mikes on a large trail like the AT. Trail names lingered in the mind much more effectively than traditional names.

"I don't have one," admitted Alex, shrugging her shoulders. "I've been hiking southbound for almost eighty days but I haven't been given a name yet."

"Eighty days, you're just a trail baby!" MacGyver laughed and his hazel eyes twinkled. "I've been hiking for like four plus months and have covered over fourteen hundred miles. Well, we'll have to work on your Trail name tonight. I got mine from a guy in Georgia because I helped him rig a fix to his tent pole that somehow snapped. I see you have a hammock. How do you like it?"

Most hikers were obsessed with talking about gear and extremely opinionated about their personal choices. "What packs are the most durable and lightweight?" and "What shelter systems work best?" were probably the two most common questions next to "What do you have to eat?"

"I do. I absolutely love it. You have to angle your body sideways in the hammock and it's incredibly comfortable. Plus, it takes me half the time to set up and break down compared to a tent."

"That's cool. I thought about using one but I opted for the tent. I have a Big Agnes Fly Creek Ultralight," the young man explained. "We're just making dinner now so come on over and hang out with us if you'd like."

"Sure. I'd like that," said Alex. "I'm just going to get my water filled and purified and wash out my socks and I'll be there soon."

Later that evening, Alex sat around a rare campfire with MacGyver, Waddles, Guano, Breaking Wind, and Teflon. Hikers rarely had the energy to light a fire and stoke it, preferring usually to hit the sack right after dinner. Hearing the men, who ranged in age from twenty-four to thirty-five, tell how they got their Trail names was pure enjoyment for Alex. Waddles, a large guy with bright red hair, got his name after running out of toilet paper and unfortunately using poison oak leaves to wipe himself. He waddled in discomfort for days. He was an architect whose wife left him for his business partner. He sold his house and hit the Trail. Guano had a bat poop on his head. He was an unemployed law school graduate who only went to law school because his father was a lawyer and wanted him to run the family firm, which he had no desire to do. He wanted to restore old homes and flip them. Breaking Wind's name needed no story since he began doing just that about fifteen minutes after dinner. He was fresh out of graduate school and had absolutely no desire to start a nine-to-five job anytime soon. He decided on taking six months to hike the Trail so he could figure out what he wanted to do with the rest of his life. He wasn't close to that answer yet. Finally, Teflon was a college dropout who had fallen six times and met with several calamities only to come out unscathed each and every time. He planned to start culinary school after completing the Trail.

"So, now you know all our stories," said MacGyver. "It's time for yours."

This was the part of the evening Alex dreaded. She was afraid of talking about her sexuality around a campfire of all men. Even though she felt comfortable and at ease with them, she didn't know them well enough to discern whether she could be 100 percent safe in their company.

She decided to start off slowly and keep her pronouns neutral.

"I'm an elementary school English teacher in Stockbridge, Massachusetts. Think Norman Rockwell painting. I found out a few days ago that I lost my job after taking a leave of absence to hike the Trail. I have an older sister Sara who keeps me sane. My dad was an Air Force pilot. He died on a training mission when I was ten years old. I went to Amherst College and always thought I'd be a writer although I barely even write in my journal." Alex was suddenly silent, thinking about the letters she had begun to write to Cate. She hesitated to continue.

"So why are you here, hiking the AT?" asked Guano.

"I needed to clear my head." Alex bit her lip and poked a stick around the fire.

"Yeah. I get that," Waddles said. "But most people go for a ride in their cars with the windows down, maybe do a weekend camping trip. Hiking the AT is a little more than just clearing your head, don't you think?"

As if sensing her discomfort, Guano leaned over and hugged her shoulders. Alex looked up in surprise. "You know, my boyfriend left me when I told him I wanted to hike the Appalachian Trail without him. He just couldn't understand why I'd want to go away without him and he couldn't forgive me for it.

So, I'm officially single in a land of heterosexual, dirty, and bearded men. The tragedy of it all."

Alex felt her shoulders relax. She was among friends. She was truly safe to tell the rest of her story. Silently, she marveled at how perceptive and real conversations with fellow hikers often were. It was as if all the surface noise was removed and what remained was a true, deep, and heartfelt connection.

"I fell in love with an artist named Cate. I met her when she was a substitute teacher at my school. We spent a great deal of time together and I fell deeply in love with her pretty early on. You know, that once-in-a-lifetime kind of love? She is the most alive person I've ever been around. Anyway, long story short, I poured my heart out to her and she basically shut me down and told me she didn't feel the same way. She took off the next day and I never saw her again. I couldn't go back to my life before her and so I did the only thing I could think of. I bought a bunch of gear and starting hiking the AT."

"Artists. They are all so damned selfish," said MacGyver shaking his head. "I dated an actor for a while and that was the absolute worst. Every freaking moment was research for her method-acting career. I couldn't deal with the bullshit."

"So you decided to hike the Appalachian Trail to get over your broken heart?" Teflon asked.

"No. I decided to hike the Appalachian Trail to forgive myself for falling in love with someone I was clearly wrong about," said Alex, surprising herself with the intensity of her response. She continued, "I used to trust my instincts. I was always so sure of that inner voice inside me. Then I met Cate and I just couldn't figure out how I could be so wrong about a person. I fell so hard for her so fast. I honestly think I fell in love with her the first instant I saw her in that classroom. I needed to do this to rely on myself completely and learn to trust myself again. It probably makes no sense." Alex shook her head.

"It makes a ton of sense," said Guano. "But did it ever occur to you that maybe you weren't wrong in your instincts at all, but maybe Cate wasn't ready to acknowledge those feelings? Maybe she wasn't ready for that once-in-a-lifetime kind of love just yet."

The thought hit Alex like a ton of bricks across her face. That thought had actually never occurred to her. Not once in all the countless hours spent hurting and wondering and wishing and walking. She had simply reverted to the singular belief that there was something wrong with her. The idea of readiness never even crossed her mind. She reeled at the idea. The cracking sounds of the campfire and the crickets filled her ears along with the heavy pulsing of her own heartbeat. The full moon glistened on all of them, lighting up the night and each of her companions in a silvery, shimmering embrace. She leaned back and looked up at the clear night sky filled with so many stars. Everyone was quiet. It was as if they all knew Alex was digesting that very thought for the first time and they were giving her the space to do it in her own way. Another gift on this long and winding Trail that Alex wasn't sure she'd ever be able to repay.

"There is a term in French that is not translatable in English: *La douleur exquise*. It's the heart-wrenching pain of wanting someone you can't have," said Teflon. The other guys looked up at him in awe. "What? I studied in France for a semester before dropping out. I did learn some things, you know," he said defensively. "I can be a sensitive man."

"I have the perfect Trail name for you," said Guano, turning to her. "Moonstruck."

"Moonstruck?" Alex's eyebrows knitted together in confusion.

"Here on this night with the full moon over us, you were struck with possibly the greatest single lesson of your life so far. There is nothing wrong with you. There is nothing wrong with the situation. The time for you and Cate simply wasn't right then, but that doesn't mean it won't be right forever. You've got about another fourteen hundred miles and a few more full moons to chew on that."

Later that night, Alex stared up at the night sky above her hammock. She watched shooting stars whirl by as if they had a vital message to deliver. The Trail had given her an exquisite gift on this night, one that she would remember for the rest of her life. She would probably never see MacGyver or Guano, Waddles, Breaking Wind, or Teflon ever again, but she would remember them always.

Alex recalled reading something about surrender once. The general idea was to surrender to the moment—not to the story through which you interpret the moment—and try to resign yourself to it. In other words, can you accept the moment as it is and not confuse it with the story the mind has created around it? That was the key question.

The breeze moved across her face, shifting a piece of hair aside like her father used to do when she was small and had fallen asleep on the couch waiting for him to return home on a Friday night after he spent the week on base. He always brushed aside the hair from her face before waking her up with "Hello, Peanut." She knew in that moment he was there with her, protecting her, watching over her. She knew that he had been watching her lug around her broken and scarred heart mile after mile, hauling it with her like an old broken-down useless piece of scrap metal. But here on this night, all the wondering and wishing and heartache simply stopped. She surrendered to the lesson and realized for the first time that loving Cate was not a mistake. It was beautiful. It was magical. It would always be so and she had nothing to forgive herself for. As the moon shone down on her, she was struck with hope most of all. Moonstruck. The most perfect Trail name ever.

CHAPTER 13

August 23, 2014 6:42 p.m.
Sharon Mountain, Connecticut

*D*ear Cate:

In those moments before I get out of bed, I become conscious of hazy, foggy moments when we are kissing or making love. Sometimes we are in Paris in January or a Caribbean island, feeling the warm breeze on our naked skin. Sometimes we're in a remote cabin with snow all around us. Sometimes we are in Stockbridge, and sometimes we are in the most remote of places. The setting changes, but the dreams of you do not. Always intensely physical. I can almost feel your lips on mine, your body pressed against mine. It always takes my breath away.

Then I force myself to push those thoughts aside and unzip my sleeping bag. I try to focus my mind on the day's tasks and the hike ahead. Yet when I have a moment of downtime, thoughts of you slip in and I am floating for a moment until I force myself to come back down to earth and refocus on my footsteps. Usually, when I think of you during the day, I'm frustrated by it. Annoyed that I can't even get through a day without thinking of you. Like it's my personal weakness.

When I reach camp for the night, I prepare a simple dinner using my trusty Jetboil stove. The food is never gourmet, but it's hot and fills my belly. Sometimes I imagine us cooking together, trying new recipes, laughing over the stove, kissing tenderly, and sharing our experiences of the day like we did during the short time we were together.

At night when I finally settle into an empty shelter or in my hammock, I let my thoughts of you run wild and free. This is my favorite time of day, although I'm usually so tired, I don't stay awake for long. I close my eyes and imagine running my hands down your body and feeling you rising up to my touch. I can imagine taking off your clothes slowly and lying down in bed with you. I can imagine hearing you call my name as we make love. I imagine feeling butterflies. I imagine feeling you inside of me. I imagine us spooning afterward. I imagine us laughing and being so incredibly connected that the world could stop and we would not care.

Tell me I'm not imagining all of this. Because if I am imagining this, if it's something in my head and not in my reality, I think it might break me. For a long time, I fought the idea that loving you had somehow changed me and made me into someone bitter and sad and alone. I don't want to be that person. I want to be the person who lights you up inside. I want to be the one to know what your lips taste like in every season. I want to know where you go when you close off the world, and I want you to always be confident that somehow you will find your way back home to me.

I love the person I am with you. I love our conversations and the ease by which we coexisted before I pushed too hard and you ran away. I love how your breathing changes when you fall asleep and how you always seem to fight sleep at first. I remember reading something from Maya Angelou. I don't remember the exact quote, but she said something like we fall in love with people and we say I love you. I'd like to be near you. I would like to touch you and hold you, but if I cannot, then I still love you no matter where you are. This is exactly how I feel for you. No matter where you are, I love you. After all these miles walked, I know that loving you did change me, but instead of railing against it like it was a curse, I know now it was a blessing. I am trying to work on myself, to become the best version of me possible. I visualize the day when we will meet again. I imagine the expression you'll have on your face. I picture the butterflies deep inside my soul that will rise again to join you. You are always on my mind. You are a part of my days and my nights. I share every breath with you no matter how many days pass between us and no matter where the winding road of life may lead. You hold my heart, and so I am bound to you forever.

I write to make these moments without you real. I write to draw the map of my love for you. I write these letters knowing that someday they will help you see. I write for myself because when I am alone with my words and this page, I'm somehow close to you. I'm beside you baring my soul to you and only you—always you.

Cate. That is my secret word. The one I whisper when I am alone in the woods. The word I form in my mouth and silently release when I touch myself and orgasm. The word is sacred to me. Your name is my lifeline. Your name is a reminder that my heart still beats in my chest.

I love you. Today and every day. Now and always. You have my heart.

Always,

Alex

CHAPTER 14

CATE

September 2014
Orleans, Massachusetts

Two weeks after Cate's dune shack residency concluded in Provincetown, she found herself almost lulled to sleep by the hypnotically gentle rock and sway of the boat. Cate's eyes were closed, and her head was tipped back against the cloth webbing of the hammock set up between the forestay and the mast. The wind was light at only two knots, but it didn't matter anyway. The sails were safely down, and Cate was anchored in the protected waters of Wellfleet Harbor overlooking the orange-and-yellow sunset on the marshes.

Her parents were sneaky, wonderful people. When her mother visited Cate at the dune shack two weeks ago, she briefly alluded to the fact that her dad stayed in town hanging out looking at boats so mom and daughter could have some bonding time. At the time, she thought nothing of it. But what her father was really doing was buying her a sailboat of her own. After her residency finished at the end of August, Cate was summoned to the Long Point Marina in Provincetown by her parents. She walked down the floating finger at the marina only to see her mom and dad standing aboard a Bruce Roberts Offshore thirty-eight-foot steel hull ketch with a big red bow on the mast. After crying and hugging for fifteen minutes, Cate's dad showed her around her new vessel like a kid in a candy store.

Cate always had a closer relationship with her mom, but her dad was a steady constant in her life. Whenever she called, he always asked how she was and said he loved her before handing the phone over to her mom for the longer conversations. But over the years, Cate realized how strong and smart her father was. He was a man of few pretenses who loved her mother so completely it was as if her mother was the sun and he was a planet orbiting around her. Not only did he teach himself to sail, but he could fix just about anything on a boat, he could make conversation with anyone he came in contact with, and he was an accomplished artist in his own right. Whenever Cate thought about her father, she always felt protected and safe, and above all else, loved for exactly who she was.

"Her previous owner cruised extensively with this yacht. It's a reliable boat you can handle yourself or with someone else," her father remarked, smiling. He was so excited to show her every single corner and crevice. "It has all new electrical, radar, solar panels, and an Eclectic Energy DuoGen wind generator, which I have to admit is extremely quiet. It's powered by a Yanmar forty-seven-horsepower turbo diesel engine with only eight hundred and thirty-two hours on it. It was bought new in 2005." Her father paused only to breathe before continuing on in an excited barrage of words. "The vessel is a substantial-distance cruising yacht with a raked stem, half-length keel, and her hull terminates in a short counter and well-proportioned transom. The deck is raised slightly from the gunnel to provide a flush deck. The center cockpit allows easy access to the main and mizzen of this ketch-rigged beauty! They also led all the lines to the cockpit for ease of single handing and safety. There is a full canvas enclosure over the cockpit." He paused again as if to catch his breath and smiled. "I've cleaned and run the engine. It looks good. No issues except a few minor wear-and-tear things I've been working on for the past couple of weeks."

Cate's mouth hung open in disbelief.

"Your mom has been hard at work getting the cabin cleaned and stocked, so you have everything you need to live aboard down to a potato peeler and new sheets and towels. You're going to love it!" her dad gushed with pure excitement and pride.

Her mom wiped tears from her eyes and said, "She's an excellent live-aboard, seaworthy vessel that your father and I hope you have wonderful adventures on for many years to come!"

Cate hugged her parents with every ounce of strength she had. "I can't believe you bought me a boat. How on earth did you afford this?"

"We are famous artists, babe," her father said with a laugh. "No really, we're doing well, and we've been saving for this day for a long time. You did us a favor by getting that scholarship to Yale, after all, so consider this a final payoff from your college fund!"

"Why don't we let Cate look around at her own pace, hon, and let her ask questions as she wants to? You're overloading her with entirely too much information," her mother said.

Cate gingerly walked around the vessel, touching stanchions and running her hand across the flaked mainsail.

"I rigged a boom preventer to give you peace of mind when you're running downwind in strong breezes," her father said when he saw Cate look down at it. He followed her eyes and continued explaining before she could even ask the next question. "Genoa foresail," he said.

"What's the draft?"

"Six feet. Comfortable cruising speed is about five to six knots."

Cate's hands touched the ropes neatly bundled along the starboard rail. "All the lines were replaced last year," her father continued.

She peeked down the companionway.

"Let's go down below," said her mom, her voice bubbling with excitement as she led them down to the interior.

The three descended the steps into the salon. Cate could tell her mother had cleaned it and replaced the fabric on the settees and added new throw pillows. It already looked so homey it brought tears to Cate's eyes. She scanned the navigation station where she saw paper charts.

Her father explained, "Even though you have an electronic chart plotter with GPS and nautical charts, and I'm sure you'll use a navigation app on your phone or laptop, you know we insist that you plot your courses on paper first."

"Never skip that step, honey," continued her mother. "You might skip a few other things here and there but always know your charts and be comfortable with your printed charts. We really insist on that."

"Yes, I know. Who do you think raised me? You guys had me plotting courses at like thirteen years old," Cate said as she peeked into the forward cabin.

"I doubt you'll want to sleep forward, so we've got it used for storage right now. We threw in an inflatable dinghy with a five-horsepower outboard in case of an emergency that's stowed there. The aft cabin is much more comfortable," said her mom.

After peeking into the aft cabin that looked so inviting with all freshly polished teak and a new starfish comforter, Cate agreed.

"We made a few improvements to the galley. We replaced the refrigerator and freezer units with two brand new Engel units. They're much more efficient to run offshore. We also replaced the stove with a two-burner nonpressurized alcohol stove. They had propane, but you're used to the alcohol, as we are. The oven wasn't working well and we just opted to remove it for you since we know the kind of cooking you tend to do." Cate's mom winked at her.

"We'll go over the engine compartment and electrical later."

"Thank God," said Cate. "I'm totally overwhelmed!"

"Good! Let's go on deck and enjoy the sunshine," her dad said.

After a week of helping her get acquainted with her new vessel and finding her sea legs again, her parents took the ferry to Boston to catch a flight back to their own boat which was currently docked in Beaufort, South Carolina. Cate was a seasoned sailor, but she would not make a trip like that right away on her own. It just wasn't prudent to take that risk. Her parents completely agreed. Instead, she planned to spend the next couple of months getting comfortable sailing on her new vessel in the local Cape Cod waters without the safety net of her parents' presence. She would dry-dock the boat for the winter in Provincetown and rent a place on shore for the winter before making a decision about sailing south to warmer waters the following spring. She felt calmer than she had in a long time and silently thanked her parents again for settling her down when she needed their love and guidance the most.

After her mother left the dune shack, Cate took to heart her mother's sage advice. She began meditating again, a practice she had honed for years but had gotten out of the habit of doing. She worked to center herself, to calm herself, and to forgive herself for how she had handled the situation with Alex. She still thought of her a thousand times a day and fell asleep each night imagining she was touching her, but she stopped beating herself up about having those thoughts. Instead, she welcomed them and shifted her mind-set, believing her thoughts somehow reached Alex, no matter where Alex might be or what Alex might be doing.

She felt her soul mending as she further immersed herself

completely in her art and sailing, the two constants in her life. Most clear mornings, she was up long before sunrise so she could have her easel set up on deck and be ready to go just as the sun peeked its yellow head over the horizon. It took her awhile to get used to painting on board the boat again, a skill she had acquired in childhood.

She fell in love again with the act of painting, with making pictures with her hands. Sometimes when she painted the curve of a wild rose flower or the white rolling waves, she felt like she was tracing the small of Alex's back or the curve of her hip. She tried to paint in the emotions and feelings of making love to Alex with every brush stroke. It was the only way she knew how to heal. She wanted to work inside the imaginary confines of her short, but incredibly powerful experiences with Alex. Those were her touchstones, and every image reminded her over and over again of how much Alex had become her home, even if she never saw her or spoke with her again. Once or twice she tried to draw Alex from memory, but she gave up because the picture in her mind's eye was too perfect and she was never quite able to capture the light in Alex's eyes or the slight slant of her smile without tarnishing what she remembered best.

After two nights on board, she decided on a name for her new home. Naming boats wasn't a task to be undertaken lightly. It was almost like naming a child, except a little irreverence was always allowed. She ordered the self-adhesive vinyl lettering in cobalt blue as a nod to her parents' boat, but the name was all hers. *Snowfall*. She named her boat *Snowfall* for the first night she and Alex made love during the February blizzard so many months before. She would never be able to look at falling snow without flashing back to the memory of their bodies intertwined and illuminated by the orange glow of the kerosene lantern. She knew it was an odd name for a boat, but it meant something intensely personal to her, and that was all that mattered.

CHAPTER 15

September 7, 2014 9:24 p.m.
Provincetown, Massachusetts

D ear Alex:
I'm sitting aboard my new home, the sailing cruiser I've named Snowfall, *to always remind me of the first night we made love. It's dark out and windy tonight, but I'm still in the cockpit protected from the wind, soaking up the dark sky and looking up at the stars. Life is short. All this time has passed that we can never get back. One day in the blink of an eye, our lives on this earth will be over, and we will have wasted so much time. I can feel it—the seconds, the minutes, the hours, the days, the months—all passing without you. They weigh so heavily on me tonight.*

I try to imagine you've received all my letters and you're on your way to me although I know that's not possible since I haven't mailed one of them yet. I try to imagine the butterflies, the tension, the feeling of coming home when you walk down the dock to me. I'm in Provincetown now at the Long Point Marina but once the first frost hits, I'll dry-dock the boat for the winter and will rent a little place in town. I know Provincetown is quiet in the winter, but quiet is what I'm after.

If only you would get here. Now. Tonight. I would tell you every-thing. I would not make the mistake I made in the past of letting silence talk for me. I have learned that lesson and will never do it again. This time I would tell you everything. I would tell you that I'm scared I'll never love anyone else the way I love you. I'll tell you that I'm afraid no matter how much we love each other we still want very different things from life. What if I can't give you what you want and need? What if you can't do the same for me? Then where would we be?

Some days are better than others and tonight is not a good night for me. I can only bury the love, the ache, and the desire for you so long before it comes barreling out of me.

I don't even know what I'm writing anymore, but the act of writing makes me feel closer to you somehow, makes me not feel so alone without you. But then, I look up and know it's all an illusion. I am on fire and burning away to nothing. Someday there will be nothing left of me or my heart but a pile of ashes and charcoal. If only I could stop thinking of you, I could go on with my life as if you did not exist or I had not real-ized I needed you at all. If only I could have stayed asleep through this life. So many people sleep through this life—why couldn't I?

I ask my guardian angels and spirit guides and God for help, for signs, to help me get back to you. I can't tell anymore if they are helping me or if all of it is a bunch of horseshit. I'm not sure if I believe in guides or spirits looking out for us, but I'm hopeful that I can have help untan-gling this mess I've made.

I miss you, but most of all I miss what we could have been together. I wish I could be the person you need. I know it would have been spectacu-lar. We would have been like comets shooting across the sky. I set sail soon and will wander until I can wake up and not think of you.

Always,
Cate

CHAPTER 16

February 2014
Stockbridge, Massachusetts

*L*ong before Cate boarded her new vessel for the first time, the wind howled outside spewing ice and snow from one direction to another back in Stockbridge. A winter blizzard was in full force, with gusts hitting upward of fifty-five miles per hour and snow falling at a rate of two to three inches per hour. The last time Cate heard the weather, the temperatures were hovering at around twenty-five degrees, but the wind chill made it feel well below zero. Cate's power had gone out three hours ago, but her loft was hovering at just barely warm enough thanks to the propane fireplace. Candles and kerosene lanterns illuminated the space, casting a warm and comforting glow around her. She dragged her mattress in front of the fireplace so she could sleep warmed by the fire.

Cate loved kerosene lanterns because they reminded her of life on the boat. Each night her father read aloud to her from Greek mythology or *The Giving Tree, Alice in Wonderland* or her personal favorite, *A Wrinkle in Time*, with the light of a kerosene lantern swaying to and fro above her bunk.

It was too dark to paint, so she sat in front of the fire on her mattress curled up under a quilt sipping a hot cup of tea. The loft was silent except for the sound of the wind howling outside. Cate closed her eyes and tried to imagine she was on the deck of the *Cobalt Blue* on a sunny summer day with the smell of salt and sea filling her senses. Just as she was settling into her little winter reverie, there was a knock at the door. Cate didn't have any friends in the area, certainly no one who would casually pop over during a blizzard. She cautiously went to the door and looked through the peephole. Her stomach lurched. Underneath a heavy parka, hat, scarf, and mittens, stood Alex looking more like a frozen Eskimo than herself.

Cate opened the door. Alex immediately started talking. "Hi, it was such a nasty night. I decided to bring dinner. Actually, that's not entirely true. I mean I did bring dinner." Alex held up a bag of Chinese food takeout and smiled. "But I haven't been able to stop thinking about our trip to North Adams and our conversation and your hand on my leg. And considering every weather report said the world might end with seventeen feet of snow and hurricane-force winds, I decided there was no place else I'd rather be than here with you."

Cate took the bag from Alex and pulled her inside without saying a word. The large wooden door clicked closed behind them. Cate pulled off Alex's wool hat, which was already dripping with melted snow. She removed her mittens and unzipped her parka so Alex could emerge like a brown-eyed butterfly from a winter cocoon. She helped her step out of her knee-high boots and chuckled when she saw the insanely bright striped wool socks Alex wore. Cate placed both of her hands on either side of Alex's ice-cold face and brushed her long hair aside. She leaned forward and kissed her fully, parting her lips with her tongue. Tasting Alex's berry-flavored ChapStick almost put her entirely over the edge. So did the feeling of Alex's tongue intertwined with hers. They moved from the doorway into the large loft space without breaking lip contact. It was as if they were two melting ice cubes floating and turning around the inside of a glass. Cate maneuvered them deftly from one side of the loft to the other without bumping into anything. She slowly lowered Alex onto the mattress in front of the fireplace and only then did they break the kiss.

Alex didn't say a word; she sighed and looked up at Cate with this expression that was so filled with passion and lust, Cate could barely keep from tearing off her clothes right there. But something inside Cate told her to go slowly as if she had to savor and remember each and every moment rather than rushing through it for a powerful payoff. Alex grabbed Cate's unruly hair and held it in a mass behind her head. They kissed again, but this time the heat was unmistakable. There was no denying the insatiable appetite they had for one another. They had danced around each other for the week following Alex's first visit to Cate's loft when they'd kissed. They danced around each other after their weekend visit to North Adams. Even though they saw one another at school, their interactions had remained professional except many secret smoldering glances and eye blazing whenever they caught a moment alone in the hallways or the teacher's lounge.

Cate's knee dropped down between Alex's thighs, and Alex responded by pressing herself harder and harder against her leg, barely rocking back and forth. The subtle movement made Cate dizzy.

Cate sat up and pulled off her heavy turtleneck sweater. There were so many layers of clothes between them. Before she could tug it over her head, Alex's fingers deftly unhooked the latches to her black bra. The sweater and bra fell in a heap. Alex quickly pulled off her sweater. The sight of a bright red lace bra against Alex's olive skin turned Cate on more than anything ever had before. The rest of their clothes went flying in all directions, and within a matter of a few more seconds, they were both entirely naked, aroused, and wrapped in one another's arms.

For the next several hours, they made love as the snow fell and the wind howled outside. The orange glow from the kerosene lantern lit up their bodies in warmth and shadow and highlighted the beads of sweat that formed as they slid against each other, feeling to Cate like velvet on velvet. Cate tried to keep her eyes open to trace each and every shadow with her eyes. They were creating a masterpiece, and she wanted to remember every detail, every movement, every sound, and every sensation.

As Cate's mouth moved down Alex's soft and supple body, Alex's rose higher and higher to meet her. Alex's body was a canvas, and Cate's tongue was the brush. Cate kissed the inside of Alex's thighs, causing her to writhe in pleasure and call out her name. Alex spread her legs apart, and Cate couldn't wait any longer. When she tasted Alex for the first time, she tasted the ocean at high tide, rainfall in the woods on a hot summer day, the first snowfall of the season. There had been other lovers with whom she failed to truly connect at this moment. But when Cate felt Alex come and her silken sweetness filled her mouth, every other lover was forgotten. Every other encounter was a mere ripple on the surface of her life. Cate instinctively knew Alex's body as if it were her own. Every shift, every rise and fall, every moan was a change in wind direction that Cate could feel as if the reactions came from her own body.

Alex turned Cate over onto her back and began kissing her full breasts, teasing her pink nipples until they were hard and ultra-sensitive. She too moved slowly, deliberately. Cate stopped thinking. All she could do was feel. Sex, after all, was an act. It was something one did, and whatever Alex was doing locked and unlocked doors she never knew she had within her. Alex's mouth expertly sucked and pulled at Cate's core causing her to quiver and convulse in pleasure but before Cate could come, Alex rose up and kissed her on the mouth, and Cate tasted herself in the kiss. Alex's fingers slipped deep inside of Cate, and the two rippled and rocked in unison with Cate clutching at Alex's shoulders as if to keep herself from flying clean out of the universe. The shockwaves they rode one after the other made Cate finally understand the concept of sexual alchemy. Both she and Alex shifted into higher consciousness, transforming, combining, and creating refined energy. Cate wasn't one to believe too much in faith or religion though she did believe in a higher power. Here in this room with Alex, Cate finally understood why she had been born. All of the wandering, all of the oceans crossed and storms passed had led her here. She finally understood how vast the universe was and how amidst the wide-open expanse of time and space, they had found one another after lifetimes or years or moments. Nothing before mattered. Nothing after this mattered. All that mattered was the here and now. All that mattered was the rise and fall of Alex's chest, the steady beating of her heart like wing beats on a red calm morning. Everything was visible, every detail meant something and, Cate knew that no matter where their lives might take them from this moment on, this would be the sum of her life. This would be the instant she remembered when her blue eyes clouded over and the world fell out of focus and time and age had taken their toll. This was the spark in the sky she had waited for on all those dark nights. Here on this darkened stormy night, they had found one another.

CHAPTER 17

ALEX

September 2014
Appalachian Trail, New York

*W*hat was passion? Passion reminded us that we were alive, that our lives were fleeting because the more intense passion was, the more unbearable life became without it. If we were denied passion, we were more than partly dead. Alex had never understood this at any point in her life before now. Her life in Stockbridge had been so protected, so guarded, and so empty before she met Cate.

She walked many miles through the early days of September with her thoughts squarely on those very thoughts. As she walked through the woods, with trees high and mighty swaying above and around her, she realized how small and insignificant she was without passion to guide her. She never knew it was possible to ache in chasms so deep inside her she didn't even know were there. It didn't matter how many miles she walked or how many footsteps she took, she still fell asleep each night wondering how she could have been this wrong about Cate and the anger rose and swelled inside her, pushing its way to the surface. As a rule, she didn't like to feel anger toward anyone or anything. She disliked confrontation, but she loathed the way she felt when her temper flared. She laughed at the memory of her mother saying she might have been British in another life. "It's like you have a stiff upper lip, and you certainly didn't get it from your father or me."

Alex also learned that the motion helped preserve her. In the quiet of an early morning or a late afternoon when her thoughts drifted to Cate, the constant motion helped stop the nausea and sickness of her own uncertainty. She walked miles trying to keep from daydreaming. She walked an entire day counting steps. After fifteen steps, she started counting again. The number was arbitrary, but it forced her to focus every thought on the steps, not on the emptiness inside her.

Until now, Alex had never felt so physically fit and strong and, in many ways, so mentally strong. And although she attacked each day's mileage with a vengeance and continued living a sparse life in the woods, mile after mile, day after day, she wavered at the mental fortitude necessary to move beyond the ache inside her that would not stop. She was so tired. Tired of being acutely aware of her aloneness. Tired of her thoughts, which replayed the way Cate kissed her or the way her body responded when Cate's hands were upon her over and over again. All she wanted to do was reach out across the divide of time and space and fall into Cate's strong, paint-spattered arms. Alex blurred out miles and almost full days daydreaming about spooning with Cate. It wasn't sexual. It was comforting. It felt like home. She could feel Cate pressed against her and she could smell the ocean on her skin. She always took care in her daydreams never to hold Cate too tightly because she knew she'd hate to feel confined and pinned down. In her thoughts, she moved away just far enough to give Cate the space she needed, but the moments that took her breath away were the ones when she imagined Cate shifting her body to get closer.

One afternoon in the middle of the rugged New York landscape, she reached Bear Mountain. The eighteen-mile section traversed the northern section of Harriman State Park, extending from the Bear Mountain Bridge at the Hudson River. She had already walked over the expansive Bear Mountain Bridge, trying to keep her focus while cars zoomed by. After spending so much time in the quiet of the woods, the rush of cars speeding by was a jarring, uncomfortable experience. She picked up her pace and nearly ran across the bridge that had looked so scenic from a distance.

After some serious climbing and sweating, she reached the side trail to the Bear Mountain Inn, which she knew was closed for renovations. She just wanted to visit it, but before she reached it, Alex simply stopped walking. She stood her ground and stared ahead of her. She slowly turned and looked behind her. The Trail in front and behind appeared to be exactly the same. She hadn't spoken to another soul in three days. She hadn't used her voice at all. A leaf slowly spun and twisted from high above her, floating down and down. Alex watched it drift to the ground. In that moment, she felt so alone and angry, she sat down in the middle of the Trail and sobbed.

Suddenly she was furious. All the anger that had been pent up inside her for months spewed forth like a volcano in mid-eruption. This was not the way she had plotted out her life. Steady. She had always been so damned steady. She stood steady when she heard the gun salute at her father's funeral. Her sister leaned hard against her, but she was the rock. She was always the rock. How could she have walked into the woods like this and expected it to solve all her problems? She lost her job and the kids who loved her and had depended on her. She simply walked away out of what? Out of some ridiculous notion that her heartbreak needed to be healed? Or maybe she just wanted the time alone to wallow in it. That made her angry, angrier than she'd ever been in her life. Her father left her. The sadness always usurped the anger. Cate left her. Up until now, the sadness was enveloped by the anger she felt. Now, it all came out in a hot, jumbled mess: the tears, the anger, the sadness, the confusion, all of it poured forth until she was so exhausted, she just lay in a heap on the ground, leaning awkwardly against her backpack in the dirt.

The trees and the sky above her, the ground and the dirt below her, had absorbed everything that spilled forth from her being. Nature had continued on, space and time still constant. Lives went on, the sun kept shining, and the earth kept spinning. A tiny translucent caterpillar lowered itself from a branch above her head on a nearly invisible filament that glistened in the sunlight. It slid silently down its self-made line and stopped for a moment as if inspecting Alex's splotchy face and tear-reddened eyes. Alex and the caterpillar stared at one another. After a few seconds, the caterpillar continued on doing whatever caterpillars do and Alex was left with a choice: either move or don't move. Either pick yourself up or don't. No one was going to rescue her here. No one was going to come out of the woods on a shining white horse and deliver her the fairy-tale ending she'd dreamed of as a little girl.

She had arrived at the place called Bear Mountain that she held this magical, mystical regard for. It was where she camped with her father the year he died. It was where all her childhood memories of love and laughter with her father were boiled down and distilled, packaged and wrapped up. This place held special meaning for her. She'd been walking for months to reach it. Yet here she was, and all she felt was anger. This was not how she expected this part of the journey to go for her. This was not how she expected to feel. Even though she knew better, it was almost as if her ten-year-old self had risen from her adult self and whispered in her ear that her father would be here in this place waiting for her. Of course, the idea was ludicrous. Her father was dead and buried in Arlington National Cemetery. But, somewhere deep within her, she believed even if she never admitted it to herself, that her father's spirit would be here and she would feel him or see him or have this special moment of connection with him. But, that's the trouble with death. There is no special moment of connection after someone is gone. They are gone, and that is that. Instead, what she felt was betrayal. Her father promised he would be with her always. He wasn't. He lied. He left her. Cate left her. The love she felt for both of them was vastly different, but the result was the same. She opened her heart to them both, and they lied.

Either she was going to have the strength and the fortitude to get it on her own, or she wasn't. The choice was hers, and hers alone. After a long thirty minutes or so, she stood up and brushed the dirt and debris from her sweaty legs. She repositioned her pack, and wiped the tears from her face with the front of her T-shirt. She had made her decision. Now it was time to get there. It was finally time to walk in the direction of the sun, and stop hiding in the shadows, nursing her wounded and broken heart.

CHAPTER 18

September 9, 2014 5:38 p.m.
Bear Mountain, New York

*D*ear Cate:

A few days ago, the thought actually occurred to me that I was finally over you. I felt like I was moving on without you. Then the ghost of you that I have concocted in the deep recesses of my heart reappeared after a prolonged absence, and I am reminded once again that I will never be free of you because my heart has put down roots and no amount of pulling will ever tear me away. I'm so angry with you. So incredibly angry and today the well of anger overflowed and poured out of me with an intensity that scared me. I'm here at Bear Mountain where I thought everything would be peaceful and beautiful. If I look around me, it is all of that and more, but the outside isn't a mirror to what's inside of me.

Early this morning while the sun was sliding up over the horizon and the night-light stars were turning off, I dreamed of you. I was leaning over a fence looking out at the water with a friend next to me. You appeared to my left and said, "Hi, Alex." I turned my head, recognizing your voice, and I jumped, startled to see you so close to me. You smiled that smile that sends shivers down my spine even at the memory of it. Then, you kissed me. I felt your lips on mine. I felt your tongue. I felt your breath. I felt your body. And when I opened my eyes, I whispered to you, still so close to your face, "Please tell me this isn't a dream." You smiled mysteriously. In my heart, I wanted so much to believe this moment was real between us. I knew I was asleep, but I hoped I was not. Then I opened my eyes, and you vanished, like you always do, the exact moment when I want to reach out and touch you the most.

Part of me hopes this dream was a message that your soul sent to mine. Part of me wonders if it's just my imagination conjuring up the ghost of who I hope you are and how I hope you feel. Either way, you are an apparition in my daily life, fading in and out of view, fading in and out of my consciousness as moments pass by without you.

Time is passing and this lifetime is slipping away. I am aware of it each night when I lay my head down that I am one day further into my life, with one less day to spend with you. The hourglass of my life has reached its halfway point, and the moments that pass by without you weigh more and more heavily upon me because there are fewer moments left in my life.

I want to say I will wait for you forever, but I am painfully aware that forever is not a promise I am capable of keeping because this body, this lifetime, is not infinite and I cannot make time stop, even for you. How could you leave me? How could you do that to me if you loved me at all? I hate that I'm so angry with you; but right now, I hate you, and I love you at the same time. How is that even possible?

Alex

CHAPTER 19

ALEX

September 2014
Provincetown, Massachusetts

*A*round the same time that Alex reached Bear Mountain in New York, Cate watched the last of her three letters to Alex disappear down the blue chute of the mailbox back in Provincetown. The moment it was out of sight she wished she hadn't sent any of them. She had saved her other letters to Alex hoping somewhere deep in the back of her mind that she'd be able to deliver them in person. She had been waiting months for Alex to reach out to her but she had not. Now Cate felt like she needed to let the past go, so she dropped all three letters in the mail at once to be done with them and the feelings they contained. She had to find a way to move on, and she had to find a way to let go of Alex and the guilt she felt.

Not once in all the months gone by had she received a text message or phone call from Alex. Not once had Alex tried to reach out to her. Occasionally Cate would look Alex up on Facebook and Twitter, but it was clear Alex had blocked her. Well, who could blame her? What was done was done no matter how she wished she had done things differently.

It was eight in the morning, and she was finally ready to depart from Long Point Marina for a day sail across the thirty miles of Cape Cod Bay to Scituate. She'd already been delayed four days waiting for ideal weather. Taking on those miles across open waters, out of sight of land for most of the journey on her first extended solo sail made her incredibly cautious. Now that the weather looked good, she was as ready as she would ever be. The idea of sailing alone without her parents there as a backup was a little scary, but she was supremely confident in her abilities and knowledge. It wasn't that she felt unprepared or not skilled enough, she had just never sailed like this without a safety net. She had spent hours poring over the charts and plotting her course. She shared that course with her parents and let them double-check her work.

Cate climbed back aboard and went through her final departure checklist. She had already spent two full days checking through hulls, hoses, clamps, rigging, sails, provisions, and electronics; charging batteries; filling all her fuel and water tanks; and so on. She had checked and rechecked everything multiple times. It was now or never. Cate turned on the engine and set to idle. She checked her bilges and made sure her GPS was set. She made her departure entry in her logbook, hauled in her lines, and slowly pulled away from the dock. It was official. She was away.

Perhaps it was all these months being land-bound, or perhaps it was just the situation with Alex that wasn't moving in any direction, but for a long time, Cate had felt stuck. Now finally with the wind in her sails and the waves hitting the sides of her boat, she felt like things were moving again. She was moving. Even if she never spoke with Alex again, she had told Alex what was on her mind, even if that telling came in a form Alex wasn't 100 percent pleased with. She doubted there was anything in her letters that could make Alex feel any differently. That was something Cate had no control over. All she could do was be honest with Alex. The rest was out of her hands.

All went well for the first three or four hours, but the weather quickly deteriorated. Cate couldn't understand where the building seas were coming from. Two to three feet was the forecast, but within hours the waves were running four to five feet and growing. She was headed thirty to forty degrees off the wind. Finally, she furled the genoa and started the engine. The choppy crosscurrent waves were getting a bit intimidating, coming from both the southwest and south. As they grew in height and the spacing between them remained short and tight—up and down, splashing over the deck—Cate became soaked. She didn't have time to go down below and put on her foul weather gear. Being hit broadside by the waves was dangerous and caused the vessel to roll back and forth from side to side. She adjusted her course to take on the waves at a safer angle.

Three times she luffed and finally got the chance to hop below to put on her foul weather gear even though she was soaked through. Everything above deck was drenched with spray and salt. She made sure her life vest was secured, and she was tethered to keep from possibly getting thrown overboard. Down in the cabin was continual chaos, but there was no point in bothering with that now. She'd deal with it later. She'd been the idiot for not securing everything upon her departure, knowing the only predictable thing about the sea was that it was unpredictable.

The conditions worsened. She called her mom and dad on the satellite phone and had to yell to be heard. She let them know it was threatening out but she believed she could handle it. *Snowfall* was taking a pounding—up-and-down waves, some of them five to seven feet. The odd wave coming in from the southwest often looked as though it'd break over the cockpit and cabin, but Cate and the vessel rolled up and over each one, spraying water as it moved. Interestingly, the bigger five-to-seven footers coming at her were the simplest to ride over. They seemed to come in a succession of threes, up and over, more like cresting swells. It was the three-to-five footers, close together and often confused, that were the worst. Those caused most of the pounding, throwing up most of the spray as *Snowfall* rode them up then crashed into the deep, short troughs before rising again.

Cate's primary concern was that she still had a few hours before reaching Scituate. She considered turning back to Provincetown, but it would be a longer ride back and that didn't make much sense to her. She didn't panic. She eventually fell into a rhythm. *Snowfall* was handling well so long as she kept her bow pointed at a decent angle into the waves, quartering them as much as possible. The angle wasn't far off her route plan, so she just endured the discomfort, watched the seas, and adapted as necessary. She hit the "page" button on her GPS to check for "Distance to Destination" more times than she cared to admit, but she finally passed the Old Scituate Lighthouse and entered the calmer waters of Scituate Harbor just after six in the evening. All things considered, she made good time, and thankfully got in before it was totally dark. She used her engine more than she would have liked, but the conditions called for it, and the vessel performed well under her. After radioing the Scituate Harbor Marina to let them know of her arrival, she was told a dockhand would be ready to assist her with her lines. Thankfully, she was able to dock without issue, even though the currents were swirling inside the marina. Once the lines were securely tied and she cut the engine, exhaustion overtook Cate. She hadn't tested herself in this manner in a long time. She was bone tired but proud of the way she handled the situation. She immediately phoned her parents and gave them the update. She heard the relief in her mother's voice. "We're proud of you, Sweet Pea. Now go get something to eat and relax."

An hour later, Cate sat down to a simple dinner of pasta and a salad, and made sure to write the details of her day in her logbook. Over dinner, she listened to the weather forecast that called for wind and rain. She'd most likely stay within the safety of the marina until the weather cleared.

Later, she lay in the comfortable aft cabin with a single light illuminating the space. The boat rocked gently to and fro, a motion that no matter how much time passed, would always be the most comforting thing in the world to her. Just a few hours earlier, she and *Snowfall* were tossed up and down the rocky sea and now everything was calm, serene, and soothing.

She listened to music and looked out the aft cabin into the salon. This was home now. But it wasn't at all what she imagined it would be. For the most formative years of her life, sailing and living aboard was home. She had it in her head that all she had to do was return to this and she would be back to her old self again, but nothing could have been further from the truth. Growing up, she shared the vessel with her parents. They were so active and alive it made the boat feel alive and special, like their own floating fairy tale. But here she was aboard her own vessel, and all she could do was think about how awful it felt to be totally alone. She'd become used to writing letters to Alex on nights like this when her mind raced to a million places, but she was done writing letters. She'd sent her last one this morning. That seemed like so long ago already. Time always had a way of moving ahead without warning or notice.

Loving Alex changed Cate so completely that she no longer recognized herself. Even when she reverted to the touchstones of her youth, she was changed. Nothing felt the same. Nothing felt complete. Nothing felt right. Cate was so out of her element here that she even considered leaving *Snowfall* docked in Scituate and renting a car so she could drive to Stockbridge the next day. Of course, she would let the feeling pass. The idea of tracking down Alex to say she was sorry made no sense at all. Soon, Alex would read her letters. It was up to her to decide whether she wanted to see Cate or not. All she could do was settle into her life again, and try to find some magic in the mundane. After all, wasn't life a constant balancing act of finding something to hang onto during the mostly boring and unexciting moments? As much as Cate wanted to be different, she knew that few moments in life would ever take her breath away. She closed her eyes and let *Snowfall* rock her to sleep.

CHAPTER 20

ALEX

March 2014
Stockbridge, Massachusetts

One morning many months earlier when winter's grip was just beginning to loosen, Alex woke first and opened her eyes slowly. She lay on her left side toward the middle of the bed, facing Cate. She'd renovated this room last and chose a blue-green color for the walls called Tranquility. Every time she woke in the room, she was both conscious and pleased with her choice. It still surprised her to wake up in her home next to Cate even though they had been spending most nights together for over a month. Cate slept flat on her back, her left arm over her head as if she was about to call for a taxi in New York City. Her mass of blond curls encircled her head like a golden halo. Alex studied the light freckles on Cate's nose and cheeks wishing she could make a map of them, like the constellations in the sky. She watched as Cate breathed deeply. In and out. In and out. Somewhere deep inside Alex, something infinitesimal clicked into place, and the sheer contentment she felt was joyous and incredibly peaceful all at once. There was nowhere else on earth she wanted or needed to be than in this quiet moment as Cate slept, her breathing filled every empty space inside that Alex didn't know existed.

Cate's almost white eyelashes fluttered. For a moment, Alex thought she was awake, but she must've been dreaming because her eyes remained closed, and her breathing continued slow and steady.

Last night they cooked together. They made beef bourguignon straight out of Julia Child's classic cookbook. It took concentration in between drinking red wine and making out for them to pull off the culinary feat. The divine smells and their laughter filled the entire house. They were so compatible. Simpatico. That was the word. Alex felt so connected to Cate. They had become inseparable, sharing almost all of their free time together. They were careful not to share anything with work colleagues, making sure never to arrive or depart together, but their relationship had progressed quickly. Alex felt like they were almost to the point of moving in together, U-Haul jokes aside.

Alex didn't want to turn over to look at the clock. She figured it was sometime around seven thirty. Because it was a Sunday, they could both enjoy staying in bed as long as they wanted. It was light as the dark and short winter days had begun to give way to the faint smell of springtime and a few minutes more of light each day. The room was cold, she pulled the blanket up a little tighter under her chin. She felt so much peace at the moment. She could have stayed there forever, watching Cate breathe, but the urge to kiss her overwhelmed her. Alex shifted and kissed Cate's right shoulder. She inched closer to gently nuzzle her nose into the warmth of Cate's neck where she inhaled a combination of powder, ocean, and Calvin Klein's Eternity perfume. Alex marveled at how Cate could smell like the sea even though she hadn't been near it in months. Quietly and without hesitation she whispered, "I love you" into Cate's ear, thinking Cate was still asleep, but after uttering the words, Cate slowly rolled over to face Alex, opening her light blue eyes rimmed in dark indigo with a look of surprise.

Cate did not say it in return. Instead, she simply kissed Alex on the forehead, then the cheek, then lightly on the lips. She wrapped her arm around Alex, tucking her in a tight embrace. Alex hadn't planned to tell Cate she loved her, nor had she given too much thought to whether Cate felt the same—she assumed she did. The truth was, Alex felt love and wanted to tell Cate. But Cate's silence was so unexpected when she didn't respond, Alex tensed and time seemed to stop. Even though Cate's arm was around her, Alex suddenly felt separate and alone. She tried to pretend she wasn't hurt…tried to chalk it up to bad timing or just morning grogginess, but there it was: Cate's lack of verbal response triggered worry and uncertainty—something Alex hadn't felt about their relationship until now.

Alex pulled herself upright and hugged her knees. She could barely bring herself to look back at Cate, whose hand was on the small of her back. "Are you hungry?" Alex asked as if nothing at all had just transpired between them.

"Starving."

"How about pancakes and bacon?"

"You read my mind," Cate said easily.

Alex rose from the bed without looking back over her shoulder. She quickly threw on a pair of sweatpants, a sweater, and her favorite fuzzy slippers. "Great. I'll handle the pancakes, you take care of the bacon.

If Alex was surprised when Cate uncharacteristically turned on the television, she hid it well. They rarely watched television unless they were snuggled up watching a movie on Netflix. Usually, they opted for classical music on Sunday mornings. Instead, Cate tuned into the *Real Housewives of New York*, on demand no less. Cate watched the Housewives, chuckling at their inane comments as she fried the bacon. Instead of setting the kitchen table, she set two places on the coffee table in front of the TV.

That's precisely when Alex knew there had been a seismic shift between them the moment she whispered, "I love you" to Cate. In a matter of moments, they went from a new couple who made love and listened to classical music on Sunday mornings to the tired, flagging couple who cooked without speaking and ate in front of the television. Alex peeked over to see Cate munching on a slice of bacon, her eyes glued to the TV. They sat there, eating their breakfast, both doing their best to skirt around the real elephant in the room.

After they polished off breakfast and the Housewives concluded, Cate stood up and stretched, avoiding eye contact with Alex. "This was great, but I really should be going. I'm almost out of paint. I need to pick up a few things and spend some time cleaning up my apartment which looks like a bomb hit it."

"Sure. Go do your thing. I'll clean up here," said Alex flatly. *Typical Cate running away when things get too real* was all Alex could think. This was like the scene at the bar on their first date on repeat. Alex was beginning to see a pattern, and it worried her.

A minute later, Cate pecked Alex lightly on the lips and closed the front door behind her. Alex drew back the curtain and watched Cate nearly run to her Outback parked in the driveway. Alex walked slowly back to the kitchen and stared at the dishes in the sink. She just couldn't be bothered to clean up. Instead, she picked up the television's remote and curled up on the couch.

Four days passed. Alex sent Cate multiple text messages. She called her. She stopped by her loft three times. Cate simply disappeared. She called in sick to work for three days and did not return any of Alex's messages. Alex fumed at home, angry that Cate was ignoring her. When Cate finally showed up on her doorstep one rainy afternoon almost a week later, Alex's temper and ego got the best of her, and they had their first real argument. Alex was so angry with Cate for simply walking away as if walking away was even an option. She was hurt although she refused to tell Cate that all she wanted her to do was say "I love you" back. She told Cate she was selfish and afraid of commitment.

"Why can't you tell me how you really feel?" Alex pleaded.

"Babe, you know how I feel."

"Then say it. Tell me you love me." The emotion was evident in Alex's voice.

"I can't just tell you I love you on cue, Alex. I'll tell you in my own time. Why isn't that good enough for you?" Cate asked, her voice rising.

"You know what I think?"

"What?"

"I think you're terrified of commitment. I think you're terrified of being tied down to anything or anyone. I never thought you were this selfish. What have we been doing all this time? Is it just fucking? Is that all I am to you?" Alex yelled.

"Is that what you think? Jesus, you don't know me at all do you?" Cate glared at her. "How could you say that's all I think our relationship is based on?"

"Are we in a relationship, Cate? Tell me. Because real relationships are based on love and the other person not flaking out and taking off for days on end." Alex threw her hands up.

"I just needed time and space. Why can't you understand that?" Cate began pacing around the room "I don't want to be attached to you every moment of every day. It doesn't mean I don't want to be with you, but I need some time to be myself and just be. I haven't even painted in like a month because I never have the time to focus."

"Don't you dare make it seem like I keep you from your art," Alex warned, her voice dropping down an octave lower.

Cate paused and drew in a sharp breath before exhaling loudly. "You've got us going here and going there, meeting Marcie and Emma, or trying that restaurant. It's not that I don't want to do those things with you, but Alex, we're not married. I had a life before you, and I have a life now. Being with you doesn't automatically erase all of that."

Alex watched Cate's beautiful lips moving but she stopped listening after the not wanting to be attached phrase. They wanted different things and weren't at all in the same place emotionally. All she wanted to do was make Cate see. If Cate could see things the way she did, they would be all right.

Thinking back, Alex should have seen the writing on the wall. Cate was afraid of permanence, of commitment. She was a wanderer and Alex saying she loved her was another nail in a floorboard designed to keep Cate in one place. But instead of giving Cate some space and freedom to make up her mind herself, Alex pressed the issue. She pressed Cate for anything that would indicate her love was reciprocated. And in the process, she suffocated Cate to the point that the only thing Cate could do was run away. No wonder why she didn't say I love you in return. Alex had given her no opportunity to do so on her own, in her own way. In hindsight, she had behaved like a teenage girl infatuated for the very first time. She became overly sensitive and sullen if Cate didn't pay attention to her the exact way she wanted at the exact moment. She left no room for Cate to be Cate.

CHAPTER 21

CATE

March 2014
Stockbridge, Massachusetts

*A*fter Cate heard Alex say she loved her, she couldn't get out of Alex's house fast enough. She was not proud of her behavior, but it came from this primal, deep place inside. Alex said the three words Cate hated hearing: I love you. The words added a layer of pressure so oppressive, the only thing she could do was run and hide. In this instance, running and hiding meant making up a lame excuse about needing paint, which she had a ton of already, and literally hiding out in her loft like a refugee for days without answering the door or the phone.

She wasn't pleased with the way she acted, but it was her modus operandi. She just did it. Over the years, she'd heard those words uttered three other times. Well, four but one was slurred in a vodka-induced bathroom stall sexual escapade that Cate never counted as real. The other three were legitimate.

The first time a woman said she loved her was in her senior year at Yale. She'd been dating Trisha since their junior year. Trisha was an accomplished pianist and composer. They met at a party and their attraction to each other was immediate. Not only was the sex spectacular, but also they generally got along and as fellow artists, saw the world similarly. She also shared most of the same friends, so it was an easy, straightforward relationship that wasn't too deep or complicated on any level.

One night they blew off steam down in the stone cellar of Anna Liffey's Irish Pub in downtown New Haven. Cate always loved the small, cramped bar because it had so much character with its bright red-and-black doors that led down a narrow staircase to the taproom always filled with Yale students and music, dancing, and laughter. They'd spent the night with friends drinking beer and dancing. And when they left the bar after closing, they walked arm in arm back to Trisha's off-campus apartment where they stripped off each other's clothes and made love with the intensity and playfulness that only comes with being partially drunk and twenty-one years old. Afterward, they lay side by side in bed flat on their backs as the sweat dried on the sheets. They weren't even touching. Cate was completely satiated and relaxed. And then she heard it. "Cate, I love you."

"No, you don't," said Cate. "You're still drunk. It's orgasm endorphins talking."

"No, I'm not drunk. The endorphins aren't talking. I am," replied Trisha matter-of-factly.

If someone were standing in the corner of the room, hidden in the shadows holding a stopwatch, they could've said it took Cate precisely fifty-seven seconds to dress and bolt out of Trisha's apartment. Hearing "I love you" from a lover set Cate's flight response to urgent and she took off faster than a 747 on a smooth runway in perfect weather. Poor Trisha. Cate never even bothered to give her an explanation. She simply cut Trisha out of her life. She stopped spending time in their usual hangouts and stopped seeing their mutual friends; she shifted herself 100 percent away from Trisha.

Three weeks later, Trisha slept all night outside Cate's door, and when Cate opened it to leave the next morning, Trisha jumped up and blocked Cate's body from passing over the threshold.

"You're not leaving until you tell me what happened to you," said Trisha with a begging, panicked timbre to her voice.

"I just don't love you and I don't want to waste any more of your time," said Cate as nonchalantly as if she were ordering egg foo young and a spring roll for lunch.

"That's it?" Trisha asked.

"That's it," said Cate.

The two never spoke again. Years later during a particularly difficult time, when Cate spent most of her time drunk and lamenting the fact she was still alone, she looked Trisha up on Facebook and saw she was employed by the San Diego Symphony Orchestra, married to a woman named Sam. They had two small children, a chocolate Labrador retriever, and an apparent love for growing award-winning roses. The next two who made the mistake of telling Cate they loved her both met with the same fate several years after Trisha.

Now here she was all over again. This time she was older, and the running away took more effort and stung a little more than it had when she was young and self-absorbed. This time, hiding out in her loft felt like hiding out like a refugee. Gone were the certainty and the illusion of complacency. Gone was the surety. Her mind wandered to what it might be like if she told Alex she loved her back, and it immediately went down a rabbit hole of feeling trapped and stuck, of being somehow stagnant with another person and those thoughts made her nauseous. It wasn't that she didn't feel as though she was falling in love with Alex. She felt it too. She felt it more than she ever did with Trisha or anyone else. It wasn't about being confused. It was the opposite, really. It was because she felt so certain. That's what scared her the most, and that's what she couldn't handle. But, instead of running away, this time she would try something different, something new. She was nowhere near ready to say she loved Alex back, but she would hang on and pretend as though everything was fine. She'd decided to pretend that Alex never said those three words, and that they simply were doing just as they did before Alex unloaded on her. This way she would have time. This way she could go on with Alex without cutting her out of her life. She'd give it a few days and try to go back to the way things were before.

CHAPTER 22

ALEX

October 2014
Shenandoah Park, Virginia

*I*n October when the crisp autumn air was fragrant with the spicy, woody smells of dried leaves, Alex sat in a worn Adirondack chair with her feet propped up against a wood railing, sipping a cup of hot and strong coffee. The Rapidan River barreled and roared just down the steep cliff from her rustic cabin tucked into the Blue Ridge Mountains at the Rapidan Mountain Retreat within Shenandoah National Park in Virginia. The steam from the coffee rose and swirled over her head, vanishing into the air like her thoughts. She was far away from Stockbridge now and anything that was familiar except the smell of winter's approach. She had walked over 1,265 miles in under five months averaging about ten miles per day. Most thru-hikers kept a much quicker pace on the Trail, but her hike wasn't about setting any speed records. Hers was about healing her mind and soul and if that took her longer than most thru-hikers, so be it. It was about the journey, not the destination.

Since earning her Trail name Moonstruck in Connecticut,

Alex felt renewed in her purpose to find peace within herself and within her heart. For too long, she fought the pull of her heart and juxtaposed thoughts in her mind. One was out of synch with the other. Instead of fighting it, she surrendered to it. She surrendered to her heart because no matter how hard she tried to be different, she finally realized the truth in the simple phrase: the heart wants what the heart wants. Her heart would always want Cate. That would never change no matter how many trails she hiked or rivers she crossed. So she let it go. She let go of all the wondering and wishing and most of all, hurting. She rejoiced in the memories with Cate and allowed herself the freedom to think of her without wishing otherwise. She finally felt healed and utterly at peace.

With that in mind, Alex was having second and third thoughts about continuing her thru-hike another 915 miles to Springer Mountain, Georgia, the southern terminus of the Trail. Over and over again she'd heard the phrase "you have to hike your own hike." Now a seasoned hiker who'd been a wandering vagabond since the end of May, she was having doubts about wanting to keep hiking. She just wasn't sure how much more she could get from her time away in this magical land of trees and trails.

Her accommodations at the Mountain Retreat were luxury compared to her day-to-day life hiking, especially for the meager price of seventy-five dollars per night. She had a spacious two-bedroom, two-bathroom cabin all to herself, complete with electricity, a woodstove, fully functional kitchen, and running water (that still had to be purified) from the stream. The Rapidan Mountain Retreat was an odd choice for her to stay at for a few nights considering it was well off the beaten path of the Appalachian Trail and the scenic and popular Skyline Drive. She easily could have stayed in Big Meadows or at one of the other lodges or cabins that dotted the 101-mile section of the Appalachian Trail in Shenandoah Park, but when she had been surfing the Internet looking for places to stay, the Rapidan Mountain Retreat caught her attention.

The camp itself was built by President Herbert Hoover, the thirty-first president back in 1929-1932 as his summer retreat away from the bustle of Washington, DC. In its heyday, the camp housed many heads of state and special guests. Now, most of the buildings were lost due to lack of upkeep or fire, but a few remained making it a scenic and historic stop on a leisurely day hike for most visitors of Shenandoah's Big Meadows region.

Alex stayed at the privately-owned Mountain Retreat, located about a half-mile downstream from Hoover's Camp, which was built at the same time by the Marine Corps to house the president's cabinet. A handful of members and nonmembers now used the camp as a home base for hunting, fishing, and hiking. The cabin had no central heat except the woodstove, so she had pulled a mattress from one of the bedrooms into the living area to remain warm and comfortable as she slept in front of the woodstove fireplace each night.

The sound of the rushing water was incredibly relaxing. Since so much of her daylight hours were typically spent moving forward from one place to another, sitting and enjoying the peace and quiet of nature in the morning without needing to pack and head out was a luxury she was thoroughly enjoying. She had promised to call her sister today, but she had absolutely no cell service at the camp. Even on the main, paved Skyline Drive, cell service was spotty at best. Her sister wouldn't worry. She had her satellite communicator on and fully charged so her sister would be able to see her exact location and send and receive text messages too.

Alex spent time reading the *Thru-Hiker's Companion*, a book put out annually by the Appalachian Trail Long Distance Hikers Association looking at upcoming sections she was supposed to hike in Virginia, North Carolina, Tennessee, and finally Georgia, but she couldn't muster any excitement or interest in what she read. In all the miles she'd covered, this was the first time she was truly ready to pack it in and go home although the thought of stopping felt a lot like quitting. Once in ninth grade, she auditioned for the school musical. It took all the courage she could muster to stand on stage alone and sing. When she wasn't chosen to perform but was selected for the scenic crew, she wanted to quit. She was embarrassed and sad she wasn't chosen as one of the actors and singers, but her mother reminded her that theirs was not a family of quitters, and if her father were alive, he would have wanted her to stay the course. Theirs was a family of doers. So, she stayed on and painted sets, which she ultimately enjoyed.

Her thoughts turned again to her father. She thought back to the section she hiked at Bear Mountain in New York. The Trail led to Bear Mountain, and she had made it there. Instead of meeting her father's spirit, she had a mental breakdown, and it rained for four days straight. Day and night, it rained. Her gear was soaked through. Her feet were sore. Her body ached, and she was so incredibly exhausted, wet, and dirty that she didn't even have a chance to dream of her father before falling into near comas every evening seconds after she zipped her sleeping bag.

She wondered what he would say if he were here now, sipping coffee with her and listening to the Rapidan River roar beneath her feet. So much proverbial water had passed under the bridge and so much time had gone by. She couldn't get any of those past moments back again no matter how hard she clung to them.

Alex heard her DeLorme inReach Satellite Communicator beep with a text message from inside the cabin. It was so peaceful here that the smallest man-made sound reverberated loudly. One of the features she loved most about this satellite system was the iPhone app that seamlessly connected, albeit with a delay of sometimes three to four minutes between texts. She simply had to pick up her cell phone and look at her text messages to see that her sister had texted her about ten times.

Sara wrote:

Hey, so I stopped by your house today.

All is good.

Picked up your mail.

A lot of crap. Two bills. Will scan and send you PDFs.

Um, you got three letters from Cate.

Alex stared at the text message. Letters from Cate? That wasn't like her at all. Alex felt her mouth go completely dry. The communicator beeped as another text came through from her sister.

Did you see what I just said? Three letters.

And no, I did not open them.

What do you want me to do?

Alex gazed up at the sky that looked like someone had taken a great big stick and swirled the clouds and the deep blue sky together. Mare's tails her grandfather had called them. She listened to the roar of the whitewater rapids below. The weather was changing. Her grandfather always said when mare's tails were in the sky, it meant rain was coming soon. She was thankful to have the shelter of the cabin for whatever the weather might have in store. Her mind swirled around much like the clouds. One moment her thoughts rested on Cate, the next on the content of the letters, the next on the formation of the clouds or the smell of her coffee. She had no idea what to do next. Should she go home? Should she ask Sara to send the letters on to her? Should she tell her to throw the letters out? She was at a total and complete loss. The messenger beeped again.

Hello? What do you want me to do?

Alex picked up her cell phone and typed a short message.

Need time to think. Will let you know soon.

She walked into the cabin and plugged her phone in to charge. She needed to go out for a walk to clear her head. In a matter of minutes, she packed up a few essentials, including water and lunch, into her near-empty backpack, laced up her boots, and grabbed her hiking poles. She began walking up the rough, pothole-laden dirt road in the direction of President Hoover's

Rapidan Camp. She'd read about it but hadn't visited it yet. After a short half-mile hike, she saw the first building. She took a left at a cement trail marker and walked over a short, curved wooden footbridge. Up to her right was President Hoover's personal cabin. It was one of the few cabins that still remained intact on the property. The deck overlooked the stream of the Rapidan River. She climbed the few steps to the deck and sat down on a roughly hewn Adirondack chair and looked down at the smooth rocks and flowing water. No one was here, and the museum buildings looked closed. It was peaceful and just what she needed. She had no real agenda for the day and nothing else to do, so she decided to sit and take in the scenery for a while.

She wondered what those letters contained, and the thought occurred to her that Cate would have no way of knowing where she was. She had blocked her from Facebook months ago in a fit of rage and they had no close friends in common. All she knew was that Cate had an artist residency in Provincetown for August. That's it. The irony was also not lost on her that Cate sent her letters and she'd been writing Cate letters too, although she lacked the courage to mail them. Part of her heart opened up at the mere thought Cate was thinking of her. Part of her was afraid of what Cate had to say. What if it was an explanation about why she did not want to be with her? What if it was further confirmation that Cate did not love her?

Alex faced the fact that she was afraid, and believed in a weird way she was almost better off *not* knowing what Cate had to say. But, nothing else would come from this limbo place she found herself in, and she had never been a timid, fearful person. After strolling around the grounds of Hoover's Camp and peeking in a few windows of the closed buildings, she walked the half mile back to the cabin and texted her sister. Her decision was made.

CHAPTER 23

CATE

April 2014
Stockbridge, Massachusetts

Six months before Alex had reached the Rapidan Retreat in Shenandoah Park, Virginia, Cate slid into a deep red banquette next to Alex at the Lion's Den, a pub located downstairs at the Red Lion Inn in downtown Stockbridge. Diva and the Dirty Boys had just started their first set of bluesy rock and roll, and the place was jumping. The Lion's Den had so much character with its dark mahogany coffered ceiling and rustic wood-paneled walls. It was a great local pub that always had eclectic live music on Saturday nights.

Her hand rested underneath the table on Alex's thigh. This was the first time they'd gone out since Cate's "I love you" disappearing act. Things were still tenuous between them, so it made sense that Alex suggested a night out with friends. Moments later, two of Alex's childhood friends waved at them from across the room and headed their way. During the past two months since Alex and Cate had begun seeing each other, Cate got to know Marcie and Emma quite well. At first, Cate was hesitant to meet

Alex's best friends, but after five minutes with both of them, she felt completely comfortable. Both were genuine and funny, and Cate saw right away why Alex loved them so much. Marcie and Emma weren't a couple although Marcie was always trying to get into Emma's pants, which had become a constant joke over the years of their friendship. Emma was divorced from a police officer and "strictly dickly" as she always so gently put it. Marcie had recently broken up with a longtime girlfriend. The trio had been best friends since fourth grade, growing up next door to each other.

"Hey, babes!" yelled Marcie over the loud music. The four hugged and quickly settled into their seats. Alex flagged a waitress and ordered a pitcher of beer. She leaned close to Marcie, away from Cate, laughing and talking with her. It was nearly impossible to hear anything they were saying over the music, and Cate felt as though Alex was ignoring her a little bit. Cate caught Emma's eye, Emma winked at her.

"Everything good?" Emma asked. Cate couldn't hear her, but she read Emma's lips. Cate nodded yes, even though things were far from perfect between her and Alex, and took a long swig of beer, shifting her attention to the band. The vibe in the bar was happy, cozy, and fun, with all the dark colors, great music, and patrons smiling and laughing. Cate couldn't figure out why she couldn't just let go and relax, but she felt awkward and more than a little uncomfortable. She continued to drink her beer as Alex talked and laughed with her friends. Alex was so animated tonight that it surprised Cate. It was as if her mood was the complete opposite of Cate's. Just as Cate was about to excuse herself for some fresh air, the band took a break and the bar suddenly became quiet, allowing for easier conversation.

"Wow! They are a great band," remarked Emma.

"They're here all the time," said Alex.

"So, what's going on, you two?" asked Marcie. "We haven't seen you guys in a while."

"Oh, not much. I just told Cate I loved her and she has yet to say anything. In fact, she disappeared on me for almost a week. This is the first time we've seen each other."

Cate was shocked. She knew Alex shared everything with her best friends but the way she just blurted out such intimate details between them made Cate immediately uncomfortable. Alex was being confrontational and Cate didn't like it one bit.

Emma and Marcie raised their eyebrows in unison and just stared at Alex. It was as if they were afraid to look in Cate's direction. No one said a word. Alex took a long swig of beer as though she'd just read out the weather forecast. Cate cleared her throat.

"Well that's a little personal," said Emma, trying to smooth over the apparent friction between Cate and Alex that was quickly swallowing the entire table.

"Well, you asked what was going on, and that's what's going on." Alex shrugged and stared at Cate as if daring her to respond.

"It's a little more complicated than that," was all Cate could manage to say.

"Is it? Really? I don't think so. I said I love you. You did not. You left and wouldn't return a phone call or a text message or answer the door when I came by multiple times to see you. And I knew you were inside the whole time, by the way. And now here we are. How is it any more complicated than what I said? Either you love me, or you don't," Alex said, her face reddening and her eyes flashing darts in Cate's direction.

"Well, here I was thinking this was just going to be another fun and carefree night at the pub with my besties. Leave it to us to have a little drama. What do you say, Emma? Want to go outside and make out for a few minutes and give these kids space to talk?" suggested Marcie as she basically yanked Emma up from her chair since she was too riveted to all the drama to move.

"Um, yeah, sure. Wait. No, I am not making out with you but yes, let's get some fresh air or something," stammered Emma as she and Marcie made a beeline for the door, leaving Cate and Alex alone at the table.

After a few moments, Cate spoke. "That was entirely uncalled for. If you have something to say to me, say it to me in private, but to embarrass me like that in front of your friends and here at the pub isn't right, Alex."

"Why not, Cate? They know everything going on between us. They're my best friends. I don't have secrets with them. Apparently, you just have secrets from me."

"Wait, what? I'm not keeping any secrets from you," Cate said, flinching.

Alex leaned in toward Cate. "Then why do you run for the hills the moment I tell you how I feel about us? What is it that keeps you from letting yourself go with me?"

"I do let myself go with you." Cate's voice took on a hard edge, and she squeezed the beer glass so tightly she thought it might shatter. She did not like the turn this conversation was taking.

Alex drew her hand underneath the table and pushed Cate's legs apart. She applied so much pressure to Cate's crotch so fast Cate jumped up, banging her knees hard on the table. Alex kept her hand in place, moving it up and down, up and down. "This is what you mean by letting yourself go? I can feel your body responding to me. You want me to fuck you here like this?" Alex didn't ask so much as demand. She deftly unbuttoned and unzipped Cate's jeans in one smooth motion and slipped her fingers underneath Cate's panties. "You are already wet. I can take you whenever I want," she said, leaning into Cate, her lips grazing Cate's ear.

"Stop, Alex. Please," Cate mumbled. Damn it she was turned on. She shifted her hips so Alex could access her further.

"Do you really want me to stop?" whispered Alex.

"No. Yes. Please, Alex." Cate rocked gently in the booth. She was beginning to tremble.

Alex suddenly pulled her hand away and stood up.

"Is this all I am to you? Someone to fuck?"

Cate's mind spun with confusion. Her body was still trembling. "Alex, wait." Cate struggled to zip and button her jeans before standing up herself. "No, that's not all you are to me."

"Prove it," Alex said as she marched out of the bar.

Cate took a second to compose herself before she ran out after her. She sped out to the street but just saw Marcie and Emma off to the left.

"She went that way," said Marcie, pointing to the left.

"Thanks," Cate said as she continued down the street.

A few moments later, Cate caught up with Alex. The two walked down the street together in silence. Cate tried to think of what to say or how to say it but she just couldn't. She hated the pressure Alex was placing on her. She felt boxed into a corner and more than a little trapped. Finally, she grabbed Alex's arm and pulled her over to face her, holding both Alex's hands in hers.

"Alex, please. Stop for a second. We need to talk about this."

"What's there to talk about?" said Alex, an edge of coldness to her voice.

"You need to understand—I'm trying. I really am. I care about you. But pulling the crap in the bar isn't going to solve anything. You can't sabotage me like that."

Alex soon softened. "I'm sorry about what I did inside. That wasn't right."

"No, it wasn't. Alex, you can't push me to say something I'm not ready to say. It doesn't mean I don't want to be with you or I don't want our relationship to grow. It just means we aren't in the same place just yet. Please be patient. There is nowhere else I want to be but here with you."

"Okay. That's fair. I don't like it, and I can't say I understand it, but I hear you." A shy smile reached Alex's eyes. "Plus, admit it," she added, "I did turn you on."

Cate's hand slid around Alex's waist, pulling her closer. "You have no idea," she answered.

"Oh, I think I have an idea. You were like Niagara Falls in a matter of seconds."

"Funny. You're so funny. Come here." Cate pulled Alex closer and kissed her deeply. "Now, let's go back inside before your friends send the police out to us."

Alex kissed her back. "You don't want to go home?" She raised an eyebrow at Cate.

"No. I want to go inside and finish my beer and listen to music," Cate said, kissing the top of Alex's perfect nose. But the ambiguity hung in the air between them like a shifting fog and wasn't about to lift anytime soon.

CHAPTER 24

April 2014
Stockbridge, Massachusetts

A week after the Lion's Den, Alex sat down facing the interior of the restaurant at Once Upon A Table, a cute bistro tucked into an alleyway in Stockbridge. This was one of her favorite restaurants in town. It was quaint, and the food was always stellar. The warm early-April evening bore the scent of spring all around. Alex was nervous. Since the Lion's Den, things had been off between her and Cate. Cate was keeping more distance between them. Alex felt her pulling away. She just didn't know what else to do, so she invited Cate to dinner with plans to give her a special gift she had been working on since they met. Alex changed her outfit three times in preparation for their dinner date to find the perfect mix of comfortable and cool, settling on her faded blue jeans and a long gray cardigan sweater. It was too warm for a jacket anyway.

Alex carried a special gift in her bag; one that she had been working on since her first trip with Cate to North Adams. It was a journal of sorts or a gift book of memories and dreams and wishes. It was hard to explain actually. She wanted to capture every moment with Cate because every single moment had been special. So, after each date or conversation, she wrote. Sometimes it was a poem. Sometimes it was a letter, sometimes she pasted in cocktail napkins or photos she'd taken. It was part scrapbook, part love letter, and she wanted to give it to Cate tonight to show her how much she loved her. Her thirty-third birthday was just two weeks away and she had finally found the person she wanted to spend the rest of her life with. It was as if all the puzzle pieces of her life had finally fallen into place. Even after the stressful night at the Lion's Den, Alex felt like they had moved forward slowly, and she was hopeful about the future.

Cate arrived right on time, a trait Alex always appreciated. Alex rose and smiled. They kissed briefly before sitting down. Every time she saw Cate, she filled up inside from depths so deep it always astonished her. Cate looked radiant as usual, her hair swept back in a long French braid that fell to the middle of her back.

"Hi. Sorry I'm late," said Cate as she picked up the cocktail menu and scanned it.

"You're not late. You're right on time."

After the waitress came and took their drink and appetizer order, Alex took Cate's hand from across the table.

"You look awfully serious," joked Cate.

"I have something for you." Alex handed her the journal wrapped with an orange ribbon

Cate looked puzzled. She took the journal and opened it, leafing through the pages. "What's this?" she asked in a tone Alex couldn't quite place.

"It's a gift. It's a journal, but it's also kind of a scrapbook. I started keeping it right after we went to North Adams. It has memories of things we've done together and shared, but I also wrote letters to you and a few poems—whatever struck me. You express yourself through your painting, but I've always expressed myself better in writing. After I told you I loved you, I felt you pulling away from me, and I realized how unfair it was for me to spring that on you."

"Well, what do you call this?" Cate asked. "Isn't this springing something else on me?"

Alex could feel the blush rising from her neck. This was not going as planned. "I never thought of it that way. I wanted to give you something that would help explain my feelings for you, and show you why I fell in love with you and how I feel for you. Cate, I've never felt like this for anyone else. In a way, I'm giving you my heart here. I thought you'd like it."

Cate continued to leaf through the book, stopping here and there to read a passage or a line. She didn't say anything for the longest time. Alex felt more and more anxious. Cate fidgeted in her seat, but her face lacked any discernable expression that Alex could read.

"What's wrong?" Alex asked. Suddenly her head buzzed. It was faint at first, almost like hearing an airplane far, far away overhead. She couldn't feel the wood-lacquered table underneath her forearms. It was as if the table, the restaurant, and the wall were all dissolving into nothing, and she was sitting alone in the middle of nowhere with nothing recognizable around her.

"I'm not any great shakes you know," said Cate quietly.

"What?" Alex could hear her own voice rising in tone, the anxiety swirling around her, turning her stomach. "That's what you have to say?"

"It's true. Look, Alex, I don't understand how you can feel this…I don't know…deeply for me. We're still getting to know each other, and honestly, I don't feel the same." Cate dropped the journal back on the table in front of Alex, and the thud reverberated between them.

Alex felt something drop deep inside her. She literally felt it hit the ground and disappear. Her feet were cemented to the floor. The waitress brought their drinks and an order of vegetable dumplings they'd planned to share. Alex smelled the sharp acidity of the soy vinaigrette that accompanied the dumplings. Against her will, her stomach grumbled in hunger. She felt hot tears well up in the corner of her eyes, but she refused to blink. She refused to let one single tear fall down her cheek.

"I don't understand," was all she could manage to say. "We've shared so much, Cate. How could you sit there and say you feel nothing for me?"

"I didn't say I felt nothing. I said I did not feel the same. Alex, I enjoy being with you, and I won't deny we have an incredible connection but I'm not in love with you. I don't love you. I don't feel that way. This journal isn't going to make me feel anything more than I already do. It's wasted on me. I don't deserve it anyway."

Alex stared at her to see if she could find a chink in her armor. The woman was so damned hard to read sometimes, but Cate avoided eye contact. Alex placed both hands on the journal and felt the chasm between them almost swallow her whole. At that moment, Alex saw a callousness in Cate she never knew existed, and it infuriated her. How could a woman who was so present when they made love be so disconnected at this moment? How could a woman who made her laugh and think and feel things shut down so completely? It was as if a single light had been snuffed out in a large, dark cavern. There was nothing left to say. Alex somehow uprooted her feet from the floor. She refused to give Cate the satisfaction of walking out first. That was Cate's modus operandi but not this time. This time Alex would leave first. She would walk away and save the ounce of self-respect she had left intact.

"I don't understand you, Cate. I don't know how you can be so cruel. I thought we shared something real together, something special, and something rare. I was there when you kissed me. I was there when we made love." Alex's voice rose to near panic even though she was trying desperately to keep it under control.

"You can't tell me you felt nothing. You can't sit there all emotionless and vacant and tell me you don't feel what I feel. I know you do. I've heard you cry out my name when we make love. I've seen the way you look at me in the morning before we start our day. I'm not crazy. Don't you dare make me think I'm crazy." Her chest felt tight, but she didn't stop. "You know what you are? You're a coward. You are sick down deep somewhere, and you are a manipulative bitch."

Alex stood so abruptly her chair fell over. The rage inside her terrified her. The few other patrons in the restaurant looked over at them in surprise. Alex grabbed her bag and stuffed the journal inside it. Her hands shook. Her whole body shook. She ran out of the restaurant without a second glance. She stood for a moment in the alleyway behind the mews and tried to figure out which direction to go. It was dark, so very dark. She ran as the tears streamed down her face.

PART II

CHAPTER 25

CATE

April 2014
Stockbridge, Massachusetts

*M*oments after she watched Alex rush from the
restaurant and down the alleyway, Cate paid the
bill for the uneaten food she and Alex had ordered before the
whole conversation went down the toilet and walked back to her
loft. She didn't blame Alex for running out of the restaurant; she
expected it. The familiar ache of something amazing blown to bits
had settled back into her chest like a cold heralding the onslaught
of a full-on flu. The evening had suddenly turned raw after the
hint of warmth from earlier in the day, so Cate wrapped her coat
tighter around her body and hugged herself against the chill. She
wasn't sure what stung more: the cold wind or Alex's words.

After a long walk home, she trudged up the stairs to her loft,
suddenly weary in a way she had never been before. She dropped
her bag and pulled off her boots and, in the darkness of her loft,
went straight to bed, fully dressed. As she lay there, she heard the
click of the steam heat pipes. The sound comforted her as if the

physical world still kicked and lurched on even when everything had stopped moving in her heart. She wondered if even her blood had stopped moving. Everything felt frozen and stiff, aching and empty and the feeling felt more familiar than she thought it would. "Coward. Sick. Manipulative bitch." The words churned around her mind in an endless loop and each time around, they stung more.

Cate closed her eyes and tried to relax, but her mind had other plans for her. This feeling, this was what she dreaded most of all. She had successfully avoided it for over fifteen years after only allowing herself one-night stands or meaningless, short-term relationships built solely on the promise of great sex. But, here it was again, as familiar as it was the first time she felt it. She was sixteen years old when she vowed never to get this close to anyone ever again. She was sixteen years old when the physical pain of heartache was so overwhelming she almost choked and drowned on it amidst the glorious white sand beaches of the Bahamas. As if it were happening for the first time all over again, she remembered the way she had lain on a large purple blanket, her feet inches away from the crystalline blue-green waters lapping the white sand beach. She turned her head and saw Amelia next to her, her eyes closed and her light eyelashes clinging to a few freckles on her cheek. Amelia was so tan, but the kind of golden tan only blondes can get. She and Cate had been in a fierce contest for the last three weeks to see who could turn more golden brown and right now, Amelia was winning easily. Cate turned onto her side and propped her head up with her hand. She leaned down and kissed Amelia on the lips and tasted the salt of the ocean.

Amelia smiled as the breeze shifted a few strands of hair over her eyes. Cate brushed them away. "I wish we could stay here forever."

"Me too," Cate said. And it began—the aching from someplace deep inside of her.

"I don't understand why you can't stay here with me," said Amelia. "My parents won't mind. They aren't even here half the time anyway."

"I can't." Cate sighed. "No way will my parents let me stay here. We sail together and we are heading back to the States finally."

"What if I never see you again?" Amelia turned onto her side so their bodies could touch.

Cate's heart raced, and she couldn't quite catch her breath. She tried to ignore it, but the feeling snowballed inside her. She had to say it. It was the first time she felt it for anyone, and this might be their last time alone together.

"I...ah...I need to tell you something."

Amelia stared into her eyes. "Okay."

"I think I'm in love with you. I mean I think I love you. Wait that came out wrong. I love you." Cate was terrified as the words left her lips. She said them. Not in the most eloquent of ways, but she said them.

Amelia rolled over and yawned. "I'm starving. We need to eat something."

"Wait, did you hear me? I just told you I love you." Cate's anxiety rose in her like a tidal surge.

"I heard you, babe, and it's very sweet, really. But I don't want to get into this whole I love you, you love me cry fest because you're leaving. So, let's get some food and drinks and have fun before you sail out."

Later that night, Cate walked around Smith's Point looking for Amelia to say good-bye before her curfew. She wove her way between bonfires and people laughing, dancing, and drinking until she finally saw a group of teenagers she knew Amelia liked to hang out with even though her parents told her to stay away from a few of the boys. As Cate walked toward the group, hidden by the darkness and shadows from the bonfires, she saw Amelia dancing with a boy named Jacob who always seemed angry and drunk and had too many tattoos on his arm for someone in his teens. Cate stopped walking because the air suddenly became still and hot and she heard a buzzing sound in the back of her head. She saw Amelia wrap her arms around Jacob's neck the same way she did with Cate. Amelia kissed Jacob hard, their tongues roughly maneuvering around each other's mouths.

Cate felt physically ill. She had just told Amelia she loved her. They promised to stay in touch. They promised to spend time together when Cate got back onshore in the States. There in the darkness, Cate saw all she needed to see and her tender sixteen-year-old heart was broken. She must've made a noise because Amelia stopped playing tonsil hockey with Jacob and peered at Cate, who stood alone in the semidarkness. Amelia stared at her for a few moments, smirking, before she made out with Jacob all over again.

The sheer power of the memory forced Cate to sit straight up in bed in the quiet of her loft. The darkness from that night to this one was almost the same, and once again, it was as if she'd been cast out of the light of the sun. She curled inward, lay on her side, and hugged the comforter under her chin. Try as she might, she couldn't will the memories to go away. One moment she remembered the sheer flush of excitement when she had sex with a random woman in a bathroom stall of a nightclub in New York City. The next, she remembered the way Alex's lips felt the first time they kissed. All of it amounted to the same pain and heartache she vowed she would never feel again. Some people might think she was crazy for altering her entire life because of a bad ending to a first love, but Cate's feelings were Cate's feelings and she could no more change them than she could change the tides.

That was the cruel joke of life, Cate finally realized. She'd deluded herself into thinking she was in control because of the countless decisions and choices she made each day, down to what clothes she wore or what music she tuned into or whether she wanted skim milk or half-and-half in her latte, but none of those choices mattered. It was the choices she made after careful thought and consideration. Those were the ones that bit her in the ass and reminded her that life would keep bringing her back to her biggest mistakes until she learned how to stop making them.

CHAPTER 26

ALEX

December 15, 2014
Springer Mountain, Georgia

*N*ow a lifetime removed from that awful day in Stockbridge, Alex passed her last white blaze on the Appalachian Trail on a cold, windy mid-December day. A cold snap resulted in little human traffic on the Trail, making the final eight-mile stretch refreshingly lonely. Alex felt as if she was the only person on earth as she passed rhododendron thickets, crystal clear streams, and pine forests. Thick blankets of pine needles silenced her last steps and the click-click of her hiking poles, an observation she found incredibly comforting.

She was officially a conqueror of the useless. The successful completion meant nothing for her career and would most likely mean little to anyone else outside of interesting dinner conversation. But to her, it was everything. She was not a quitter. That was the predominant thought in her mind as she climbed to the top of Springer Mountain, the Appalachian Trail's southern terminus since 1958, 3,782 feet up.

Alex walked 2,180 miles over seven months and fifteen days.

She went through eleven pairs of hiking socks, two pairs of hiking boots, and one pair of sneakers. She changed her gear six times to handle the changes in season and location. She burned around 900,000 calories, fell sixteen times, was stung by bees five times, saw four bears (one followed her like a puppy for close to a quarter mile until she blew her safety whistle repeatedly at him), lost a total of twenty-seven pounds, picked off countless ticks, warded off giardia twice, and somehow in the middle of all of it, found out who she really was.

She heard a noise and lifted her head only to see her sister Sara, her mother, Marcie, and Emma at the Springer Mountain Terminus marker, holding up plastic cups filled with champagne and wielding cameras to capture the moment. She had not expected them or anyone for that matter. She expected to finish the Trail the way she started it: on her own. But there they were, her family, her best friends: the people she could count on most. They were there to celebrate with her. She dropped her hiking poles and unstrapped her pack, letting it fall in a heap behind her. She ran to them, not caring about the way she looked or smelled. She ran into their waiting arms and let them envelop her in the single best embrace of her entire life. Champagne spilled all over her head. She laughed. Her mother looked out of her element, and that made Alex laugh harder. She also laughed at the way her mother stared at her—as if she had just returned from a long incarceration as a prisoner of war.

"Baby sister! You did it. We are so crazy proud of you right now!" said Sara as she handed her a plastic cup sloshing with champagne. "I always knew you'd do it. You were so determined."

Alex looked at the ground and saw a picture. "What's that?" she asked.

"Oh, we brought Dad along. We figured he'd want to be here with us."

"You have amazed me. Absolutely amazed me," said her mother, squeezing her arm. "I can't say I'll ever understand it, but wow, Alex. Your father would be beside himself with pride if he were alive to see this."

"You did it, babe! I love you so much!" Marcie said, gushing.

Emma was too busy crying to say a word, but she kept hugging Alex over and over again.

Alex started to cry right there. And it wasn't just a few tears. She did the full-on ugly cry. Her father had been with her the entire way, in her darkest moments and brightest days, but seeing that picture, her mom, Sara, Marcie, and Emma meant more to her than just about anything else ever had or ever would.

"So how do you feel?" asked Sara as she gently wiped away her sister's tears.

"Hungry," said Alex. "Starving actually."

"Ahh, we figured as much. I brought you a sandwich with chips and a soda. Hang on," said Emma finally.

"The two words chips and soda are music to my ears!" said Alex, laughing.

Emma rummaged around her backpack and pulled out the food. Alex sat down where she stood and inhaled everything in what seemed like seconds.

"Slow down, dear. You'll get gas. Remember that time I had to take you to the hospital because you drank all that soda? They thought you had appendicitis. You just had gas from all the bubbles in the soda," said her mother.

"Oh, Mom, I've missed you," mumbled Alex, her mouth full.

After she finished eating, she grabbed her pack and hiking poles. They still had to make the descent from the summit.

"Where did you guys park?" asked Alex.

"We parked just off Big Stamp. It's a little parking area about a mile from here. It was the closest place we could park and meet you," Marcie said.

Alex looked out one more time at the view from the summit, which wasn't terrific on such an overcast day. Her sister quietly approached her and handed her Cate's letters.

"Here," said Sara. "You asked me for these if you finished the Trail. Well, you finished the Trail."

Alex glanced down at the envelopes with Cate's sprawling handwriting and looked at her sister with surprise.

"We are going to get a head start down the access trail. Just catch up when you can. We'll give you some space." With that the four women walked off, leaving Alex alone on the summit with Cate's letters. She once again unstrapped her pack and dropped her poles to the ground. She sat cross-legged, staring at the letters as if trying to decide whether she should read them or simply throw them off into the woods. She'd known about the letters since her sister told her about them way back in Virginia's Shenandoah National Park in October. It seemed like a lifetime ago. Since then, she'd walked almost 916 miles with the knowledge that Cate had written to her and without knowing what Cate had to say in those letters. Some days all she did was imagine that Cate professed a deep and undying love for her. Some days all she did was wish the letters had been lost or destroyed. Not a day went by through Virginia, Tennessee, and into North Carolina that she didn't think about those letters or the messages from Cate they contained. The irony that she completed the Appalachian Trail just two days after Cate's birthday also wasn't lost on her.

Now here she was with Cate's letters in her hand. The envelopes were bright white and her dirty fingers had already left brown splotchy fingerprints on them. The more she turned them over in her hands, the more brown marks appeared on the envelopes. The wind had begun to blow harder and Alex was already getting chilled from inactivity and a slightly sweaty base layer. She couldn't stay up here much longer and truthfully, her longing for a hot shower almost outweighed her longing to read the letters. Almost. Alex opened the letter with the earliest postmark and began to read.

CHAPTER 27

CATE

December 2014
Provincetown, Massachusetts

Three days after Alex completed the Appalachian Trail in Georgia, the Provincetown winter wind whipped at Cate's face, nearly unwrapping her scarf and sending it into the waves. It was a cold late afternoon, and the sun had already set at just after four o'clock in the afternoon. The water and sky were the exact same color gray, matching her mood.

Sometimes her small one-bedroom apartment was just too confining to stay in all day and night, so she forced herself to go out for frequent walks. She'd heard stories about Provincetown in winter. Known as the "dark period" by many locals, it was a time when most shops and restaurants were closed, and Commercial Street was peaceful and vacant. The days were short, and the town felt cut off from civilization. It was also a time when the winds whipped so ferociously off the water, people said it actually wailed like the ghost of a whaler's widow. Cate wouldn't have believed it if she didn't hear it with her own two ears. The wind was wailing and moaning across the Bay, making the hair on the back of her neck stand straight up.

The light was the bonus for braving winter in Provincetown. In winter, the light was somehow bluer and truer than any other time of year. Since not many people were out walking beaches day or night, the wide expanses of beach were swept clean of footprints, looking more sprawling, smooth, and serene than any other time of year. The view just after the first snow at Race Point Beach was one of Cate's favorite scenes to paint. Snow and sand mixed against the clear reddish hues of sunset over the blue-green waves, making for a perfect backdrop.

She hadn't painted at all today. Instead, she tried to remain productive by cleaning her brushes and her apartment. The truth was, she felt anxious and a little off-center. Up until today, she'd felt grounded and calm. After sailing around Cape Cod and the islands until late October aboard *Snowfall*, she dry-docked and shrink-wrapped the vessel and found a small one-bedroom rental on Commercial Street in the heart of Provincetown. Her apartment was around 450 square feet, much larger than her boat. It looked out over the water from the second floor, and had the added bonus of a propane fireplace that made it cozy and comfortable in cold weather. She was walking distance to the few shops and restaurants still open, as well as the post office. She normally caught a ride or took a cab to Stop and Shop once every couple of weeks.

Her life was simple and straightforward with not a lot of clutter or confusion. It had given her plenty of time to paint, and she was incredibly happy to sell five pieces she created while on her residency, easily funding her winter rental and expenses, giving her the peace of mind she needed to continue to sell to the local galleries well in advance of the upcoming summer tourist season.

Cate walked as the wind numbed her cheeks. She couldn't quite put her finger on her unease. It was this nagging, aching feeling that left her fidgety and unable to concentrate. The gray early evening reflected back at her and didn't do anything to help brighten her mood. She could only take fifteen minutes on the beach before the damp wind was just too much for her so she returned to her apartment to make a hot cup of tea and sit in front of the fireplace. Just as she sat down with her tea and Dallas Greene's hypnotically calm voice emanating from the wireless Bluetooth speaker, she heard her phone beep with a text message. She assumed it was her mom, who texted her several times a day. Cate absentmindedly picked up the phone and barely glanced at it. Suddenly, she saw the name flash on her phone. Alex McKenzie. She dropped the phone as quickly as she had picked it up. She nearly let go of her tea but had the presence of mind to put it down on the coffee table first. It had been eight months since she and Alex had stopped talking. Eight months felt like a lifetime. She was a different person. How could she not be? She was perplexed as to the timing of this text from Alex. Her last letter was dropped in the mail to Alex way back in September. She'd not seen or heard from her since that awful day in the restaurant when Alex had shared her journal.

Cate picked up the phone again and slid the toggle over to access the text. It was simple and so very Alex. It read:

Hi. It's been a while. Would you be interested in talking?

Cate stared down at the green bubble and white writing of the text. She thought for a moment and texted back: *Hi. Yes.*

Alex responded immediately. *Where are you?*

Provincetown typed Cate.

There was a slight pause before Alex responded: *Great. I'll come to you. How is tomorrow?*

Cate was shocked. First of all, she thought when Alex meant talk that she meant talk on the phone. She never imagined she'd want to see her in person. Second, tomorrow was a Wednesday. Alex was at school or should be, and the drive from Stockbridge to Provincetown was at least four hours, depending on traffic.

Cate took a deep breath and looked around her apartment. Alex would be here. Tomorrow. Cate typed back. *Okay. I'm at 347 Commercial Street, second floor.*

Alex typed back immediately: *See you later in the day. I'll text when I'm close.*

Cate dropped the phone and looked out her sliding glass windows. The water was just fifty feet away, but because of the darkness and fog, it could have been fifty miles. She had no idea what she would do for the next twenty-four hours until Alex's arrival. Her earlier anxiety was nothing compared to the anxiety she now felt. Her stomach churned, and her mind raced. Why would Alex want to speak with her now, and what could she possibly have to say to her? Cate sat back on the couch and sipped her tea, which was now cold. More importantly, she had to figure out what she wanted to say to Alex. Over the last few months, she had thought a lot about what she wanted her life to look like. Every time she thought of an existence without Alex, she felt the heavy burden of sadness upon her shoulders. But no matter how she tried, she could not imagine a future together, one that allowed them each to have the life they wanted. She tried to imagine living with Alex in a home in the country and knew she'd never be able to do it. No matter how much she envisioned Alex sailing the world with her, she knew Alex would never be at home on the water the way she was.

She tipped her head back against the couch and closed her eyes. This was not going to be easy.

CHAPTER 28

ALEX

December 2014

*A*lex boarded Delta flight 1065 nonstop from Atlanta to Boston's Logan Airport at six o'clock in the morning on December 19, 2014, five days after completing the Trail. The flight was on time so she would hopefully arrive in Boston at nine thirty. This meant she'd have about five hours to deal with baggage claim, rental car, and a three-hour drive out to Provincetown to meet Cate in the afternoon. As she raised the window shade of the airplane to look out at the tarmac, she wondered again why she even suggested meeting her in Provincetown. They could easily have spoken on the phone. Cate most likely had no idea Alex was coming in directly from Georgia.

After spending a few blissful days eating and relaxing in Georgia, her mom and sister needed to get back to work and life in Massachusetts. After all, it was only two weeks until Christmas, and everyone was always running around this time of year. They had taken a flight out the day before, but Alex hesitated because she wasn't ready to go home yet. She had unfinished business with Cate, and she wanted it dealt with before she walked through her own front door. It took Alex an entire twenty-four hours in the Hilton Hotel near the airport to work up the courage to text Cate. An entire day of her life was wasted in a nondescript vanilla hotel room box as she prepared herself for any kind of communication with Cate. So much of her world had been spent communicating with Cate within the confines of her own mind that the mere thought of a real interaction terrified her.

Now here she was on an airplane, breathing in the stale recirculated air, wishing she were in the woods walking silently through pine forest thickets. The noise and the traffic overwhelmed her. Two hours on a plane and four hours in a car was not particularly appealing either, but the end game was. She would see Cate and figure out if what they had so many months ago could be salvaged. Before she flew out, she made a reservation for a night at the Sage Inn because she didn't want to presume anything. The only thing she knew for certain was that she wanted to move slowly with Cate. Everything was such a whirlwind when they met last January. Alex knew this time it would have to be different. This time she needed to give Cate enough room to dictate the pace.

For most of the plane ride, Alex mentally rehearsed what she wanted to say. She made a promise to herself that she would not get angry, no matter what Cate said or didn't say. She was beyond anger, and if the Appalachian Trail had taught her anything, it was patience in the face of discomfort. She would remain patient, but she would also be honest.

From the airplane seat to the car seat, Alex tried to imagine how she would feel to once again see Cate face-to-face. She had long since memorized her round, lightly freckled face; her clear blue eyes rimmed in indigo; and her strong, lithe body. As mentally prepared as she was for their interaction, she had lost sight of one thing: the way her body would physically respond to Cate. It was one thing to imagine Cate or remember moments they shared together, even if those moments were intensely physical; it was entirely another to recall the exact physical response she had whenever she was close to Cate. That was the part she could not will her memory to recapture.

Time. Time had a funny way of moving. When we're small, time is stretched out on this gigantic, seemingly endless highway of possibility. Each day, each hour ticks on as if in slow motion. A lifetime is lived between summer and Christmas Eve. Another lifetime passes from morning until night. But as we age, time constricts, sometimes as if it's cutting off almost all of the blood flow to our hearts or our brains or both. The pain is slight, a pinprick of regret that can grow into something larger, something harder to explain or acknowledge in those silent moments before we start the day or end it.

It felt like yesterday when Alex's world consisted of a classroom filled with other people's children laughing and crying, sneezing and scraping their chairs against the cold linoleum floor. A blink of an eye before that, she was nine years old eating an ice cream cone at an air show, trying to follow her father's F-22 fighter jet with her eyes at it careened off the bright blue sky. Her dad sometimes flew at air shows for fun. He often shared the skies with the Blue Angels and the Air Force's precision parachuting team Wings of Blue. She remembered the *oohs* and *aahs* from the crowd, and how proud she was they were watching her father career through the air. She remembered the ice cream dripping down her fist, down her forearm to her elbow as she stared at the sky, watching him do flips and turns at lightning speed. When her father landed and bounded down the tarmac in his olive-green flight suit toward his little girl, she believed he was a god, strong and powerful, handsome with his shining black hair and bright blue eyes. Nothing could ever happen to him. He was so strong. His smile lit up Alex's entire world. As he grabbed her up into his arms, she dropped the rest of her ice cream cone. His laughter filled her ears, and his stubble scraped her pink cheeks. Moments later, he was gone forever, a golden recollection in a glass memory case of dozens of days gone by.

High school highs and lows, college parties and hangovers, all-nighters studying at her desk, all of it filled the spaces of who she was, but none of it filled the well of who she hoped to be. The problem with Alex was that for the first time in her life, what she felt for Cate teetered on the dangerous precipice of regret. She had tried to live her whole life avoiding regret like the plague, but here it was, right in front of her. She regretted the way things ended with Cate. She regretted the way she handled the situation. She regretted jumping into an "I love you" before she knew Cate was ready. She regretted all of it. And the last thing she wanted to do was wake up tomorrow or the tomorrow forty years down the line and feel the vice-like grip of time squeezing the juice out of her very soul.

Hours later, Alex pulled up in front of Cate's rental house. The moment she opened the car door, she kicked herself for not wearing more layers. It was raw, windy, and cold in Provincetown and the wind smacked her wholly in the face as if to wake her from her daydreams and travel coma. Her mouth was already dry, and she hadn't even knocked on the door yet. As she climbed the flight of stairs of Cate's rental within the clapboard multifamily house, she noticed something taped to the door. She looked down at the address on her phone one more time to make sure she had the right place. She did. As soon as she reached the door, she recognized Cate's handwriting. It was so distinct, so open and loopy and slanted. The note read: "Alex, I'm next door at the Squealing Pig."

Alex puzzled at the note. She'd texted Cate her arrival time earlier. She had come all this way just to be sent over to a bar; however, as Alex descended the steps, she admitted that a cocktail would help calm her nerves. She walked just two buildings down before seeing the sign for the Squealing Pig. She peeked through the large picture window and saw Cate sitting alone at the corner of the empty bar, sipping a bottle of beer. She knew immediately it was Cate by the curve of her hip and the dazzling long curly blond hair that now fell past the middle of her back. The mere sight of Cate so close sent shivers up and down her spine and made her dizzy. Even takeoff and landing on a jet airplane didn't feel like this. Sweating despite the cold air, Alex began to shake. How could she walk into the bar this way? She looked around and found a bench across the street. She ran to it and sat down, gulping air as if she had just run a marathon in record time.

Alex wrapped her fingers around the arms of the cold wrought iron bench. She squeezed so tightly her knuckles turned white as she dipped her head down between her legs to avoid passing out altogether. For all her thought and all her preparation and all her miles walked, she did not expect to feel as though she'd been hit in the stomach by a cannon at short range at the mere sight of Cate. Cate hadn't even seen her yet. They hadn't even made eye contact, and yet here it was. Alex's body told her everything she needed to know: it didn't matter how much time had passed or how "over it," Alex thought she was, she was still head over heels in love with Cate. Once, a long time before, Alex had opened her heart to Cate and allowed her to see that love for exactly what it was, but Cate turned and ran the other way. There was no way Alex could walk into the Squealing Pig bar that open and vulnerable. So, she took the few moments she needed to settle down and mount just enough of her flagging defenses to feel protected.

When she felt remotely like a human being again, she stood and held her head up as she crossed the street one more time and opened the door to the bar. It creaked open, and Cate turned to look. Even in the dim light, Alex saw Cate's blue eyes shining at her. The two held a gaze for a few long seconds as Alex stood frozen in the doorway. Cate rose and Alex took a small step toward her. Cate smiled that thousand-megawatt smile Alex saw the first day they met in the art studio, and right there in that simple moment, she fell in love with Cate all over again.

Alex walked the few steps to Cate, but she wasn't sure whether she should hug Cate, kiss her, or shake her hand, so Alex simply stood there, her arms limp at her sides. It felt like forever but was just a few moments before Cate closed the distance between them, wrapping Alex so tightly and deeply into a full body hug that she had no choice but to relax completely in Cate's embrace. The two stood there, holding each other for what seemed like hours. Alex smelled the salt in Cate's hair, and the familiar scent of Calvin Klein's Eternity made her heart lurch more than once. Cate did not let go, so Alex held on. It was as if the world had stopped rotating, the noise of the televisions in the bar disappeared, the wind outside stopped blowing. Even the tides stopped moving for just a moment during their embrace, so that the months and the miles between them melted away like permafrost on the first warm day of spring.

Cate finally broke the contact between them and pulled her by the hand to a bar stool. Alex was thankful for the prompting. She wasn't sure she'd make it that far without Cate's cool hand guiding her.

"Hi, sorry about meeting at the bar, but I thought it would be, ah, safer," said Cate.

"Hi. That's fine. I could use a drink," responded Alex. The bartender overheard since they were the only two people inside.

"What can I get you?" he asked.

"I'll have a Ketel One martini a little dirty please," Alex said. She needed something strong. She tried not to stare at Cate but every time she glanced at her, Cate was staring back, her eyes large and luminous. It was as though Cate was inspecting her, trying to take in every little detail. Alex became increasingly uncomfortable with the attention as if all of her faults and scars were there on a silver platter for Cate to study and catalogue.

"You look amazing," said Cate, her voice genuine and sweet. "How are you so tan in December? And fit. You look like you've just run a marathon in New Mexico."

"Close. I just flew in from Georgia this morning. I've been away for a while. On a trip in a way." Alex stumbled. She had absolutely no idea how to explain her hike to Cate.

The bartender delivered her martini and Alex took a long sip. She immediately felt the smooth vodka slide down her throat and warm her belly almost quelling the butterflies within.

"I'm not sure what that means. How can you go on a trip in a way?" Cate asked, tilting her head to one side.

"I, uh, just finished hiking the Appalachian Trail." Alex felt self-conscious, like a young girl introducing herself to her classmates on her first day in a new school.

"The Appalachian Trail?" Cate's eyes widened. "Isn't that the Trail from that book *A Walk in the Woods*? It's really long. Like really long."

"Yes. That's the one. It is really long. Like two thousand one hundred and eighty miles long. Like thirteen states from Maine to Georgia long," Alex said slowly. Why did she feel like she was underwater? As if Cate's voice was a million miles away and she was somehow disconnected from her own body?

Cate stared at Alex in disbelief before asking, "How long did it take you?"

"Seven months and fifteen days to be exact."

"What about work?" asked Cate, still incredulous.

"At first I took a leave of absence but then they let me go."

Alex could see Cate doing the math in her head. She could see the wheels turning in her mind. Rather than jump in and try to explain, she let the words fall into the cavern she felt growing between them. Alex rested her two hands on the soft, worn edges of the bar, calmed by the steadiness of the wood. She could hear her words reverberate off the dark walls of the bar and off Cate's heart. Suddenly Alex felt like this meeting was a bad idea. Too much time had passed, too much thinking and wishing and wondering for both of them. It just had not been their time. Now Alex felt their timing was off once again and she could sense the discomfort rising within her like a rogue wave on a mostly serene day. Every fiber of her being wanted to run as fast as she could in the direction she had come. She felt her lungs constrict with a vice-like tightness. The instant she stood to leave Cate simply placed her hand on top of Alex's in an extraordinarily gentle gesture. Alex stared down at their hands. "Alex," Cate said so quietly it was almost a whisper. "Alex. You never got my letters," Cate said it as a statement, not a question as if the time Alex was away explained a great deal.

Alex sat back down on the bar stool. She stared at the bottles lining the mirrored shelves. She thought about what to say and how to say it. Cate patiently waited, her hand still on Alex's. Alex began slowly. "My sister told me about your letters about three months ago, but I was in Shenandoah National Park, Virginia. She'd been keeping an eye on my house, gathering mail, that sort of thing.

"I thought a lot about reading them, but I decided I needed to finish hiking the whole Trail before I did. I can't explain why so don't bother asking. It was just something I felt I had to do before I was ready to read what you had to say. My sister brought them with her to Springer Mountain in Georgia where the Trail ends. I read them there on my final day atop Springer Mountain. It took me a few days to decide what to do, but I decided to come here right away. I haven't even been home yet. Actually, I haven't seen my house since May. I came straight here to see you."

"Let me get this straight. You decided to hike the Appalachian Trail. It took you over seven months. You haven't been home in seven months, and you lost the job you loved?"

"Yep, that pretty much sums it up." Alex shook her head. "I needed to get away," she said wryly.

Up until that point Alex stared ahead as she spoke, but she finally looked directly at Cate as a few stray tears slid down her face. "I came to see if we could fix what was broken."

"You mean before I broke it?" Cate said, her voice barely above a whisper.

Alex wiped away her tears. She would not cry in front of Cate. "Cate, what happened between us wasn't all your fault. It took me a lot of walking to figure that out. I bear equal responsibility. I pushed you too hard too fast. I knew deep down you were scared and I pushed anyway. I was just so sure." Alex pulled her hand from underneath Cate's and sipped her martini. "The more I sensed you pulling away, the harder I pushed."

Cate sat silently for a few moments. Alex could see her processing everything she had said, but she hadn't said everything. She didn't tell Cate she still loved her. She didn't tell Cate she missed her so desperately her heart wouldn't beat properly without her.

"Your letters," continued Alex, "made me think there was a chance we could start over again."

"Alex, I sent those letters three months ago," started Cate, but Alex interrupted.

"Does that mean that's it, you're done and no longer feel anything you wrote?

"No," said Cate carefully. "That's not what I'm saying. How do we keep from ending up right back here again?"

Alex considered her words. It was a valid question and something she had also wondered.

"I'm not sure," she said. "I won't push as hard?"

"When you look at me, what do you see?" Cate sat motionless, her eyes serious. "Honestly. Tell me honestly."

Alex paused. This was the moment she had to decide whether she could be truly vulnerable again or if she needed to put up a wall of protection. She took a deep breath and looked squarely into Cate's deep blue eyes rimmed with a darker indigo before she spoke. "I see the love of my life." The truth and simplicity of the statement surprised Alex as much as it seemed to surprise Cate.

"Oh, Alex." Cate sighed. "The problem is I don't trust myself completely that I won't hurt you again. And I can't bear to hurt you the way I did. You want it all. You want the house and the white picket fence and the dog. Maybe kids? Barbecues on the Fourth of July and pumpkin picking in the fall, cutting down a tree at Christmas and singing carols around a fire. You want a home like that. I know you do. And you deserve all of it. You deserve someone who can give you all of that and so much more."

Alex nodded in agreement to the kids, and the picture Cate painted with her words. She did want children someday, but they had never even discussed that. She wanted everything Cate had said, and she wanted it with her.

"No matter how much I try to envision a life with you, I just can't see myself living that life Alex." Cate stammered. "I...I care about you so much. My heart breaks at the idea you walked for seven months just to heal from what I did to you. I can't bear the thought of doing that to you ever again, but I can't bear the thought of being tied down to a life like the one you want."

Alex felt a cold shiver slide up her spine and settle in the base of her neck. There it was. There was the truth of the matter. They were beyond a casual flirtation or a passion-filled fling. And they were in different places. Somehow, in the blink of an eye, they passed from a brief, intense connection to this. Love was not enough. Cate was still incapable of saying she loved Alex now. Throughout Alex's whole life she thought love would always be enough. She was the fool who loved sappy romances because they always had a happy ending. Love always prevailed. But here was the truth of the matter. They wanted different things from life and loving each other would not bridge that gap no matter how much either of them wanted it to.

"You know there were whole weeks that all I did was imagine seeing you again. I'd walk for hours imagining what it would be like to be near you. I believed in my heart that all of the things that pulled you away from me would disappear and we would be able to start again. Slower this time, but we'd find a way to figure it out. But it seems like you have it all figured out already," said Alex, a tinge of resentment rising in her voice that she quickly shut down. She would not lose her temper, and she would not get angry. She had promised herself that much.

"Why isn't it possible for us to try to do this together? To take baby steps if we have to but try to compromise and make it work?" Her eyes met Cate's as she continued. "I know you believe I'm this homebody who wants to live in the town I grew up in and never leave but, Cate, I've changed. I haven't seen my little house that I love so much in seven months. Instead, I chose to spend all that time living in strange and sometimes not-so-comfortable places. I'm not the same person I was the last time you saw me. I understand now what you love about exploring and traveling and being free from the constraints of a regular job and home and life. I get it now. Why can't you give me the chance to do that with you? Because I want to try."

This was it. Alex had put all her cards on the table in the only way she knew how. She was completely honest and forthright, and she'd said what she came here to say.

Cate started crumpling up her cocktail napkin with her strong fingertips. "Because, Alex, I know you. And I know me. You might want to explore and move around now but the day will come when you will want to go home. And the day will come when I won't. And we'll be right back here.

"But imagine the journey, Cate. Imagine everything in between those two points." As Alex spoke the words, she could feel Cate pulling away again. She watched Cate's eyes change from royal blue to stormy sea blue in a matter of seconds, and she knew this trip was a complete and utter failure. Cate wouldn't budge from her position and Alex could not force her. It was as if they stood on opposite sides of the Grand Canyon.

"Well, then there's no point in belaboring this is there? You clearly have your mind made up, and no amount of pleading is going to change it." Alex stood and pushed the bar stool out behind her. Her voice wavered and her eyes filled with tears she fought to hold back. "Why did you even bother telling me you wanted to talk then? Was it for closure? For you to get one last look before we said good-bye for real this time?" Alex wanted to understand Cate and for the life of her, she could not.

"How could you say that?" Cate's voice rose an octave. "Don't you understand how much you mean to me? Don't you see that I'm hurting as much as you are?"

"Then, Cate, let's figure it out. Why are you so damned stubborn? You don't have all the answers. Neither do I, but why can't we try together?"

Alex stopped. It was as if she was beating a dead horse and it wasn't pretty. She dug out some cash from her pocket. She dropped the cash on the table and looked hard at Cate. "I love you. I love you with all my heart. I want to spend the rest of my life with you. That hasn't changed in all the miles I walked. But, I don't want to be with someone who won't even try or who can't even say I love you back."

"Can't you see that this all just makes me feel more trapped?" Cate's breaths came in short bursts. "I care about you so much, but that feeling won't simply go away." She shook her head. "I don't know what's wrong with me."

"Jesus, I thought I was stubborn. My mother always told me I was. You're at a whole other level. You think you have all the answers. You think you know how the story will end but you don't, Cate." Alex paused. She reached out and brushed a stray curl from Cate's face. "Someday maybe you will see that." Alex's voice became firm. "I've got to go."

"Wait, where are you going?" Cate's eyes opened wide. "You can't leave now."

"There's nothing left to talk about. I've said what I needed to say and you've said what you needed to say. What else is there, Cate?" Alex looked down and saw tears streaming down Cate's face. Before she could stop herself, she wiped away the tears with her thumb and tasted them. "You belong near the sea, Cate. You taste like the ocean. You always did."

Without another word, Alex turned and walked out of the Squealing Pig bar as night settled in Provincetown. She hugged herself against the stiff December wind and walked to the Sage Inn for the night. She was so tired but tomorrow was a new day, and she had no idea what it had in store for her. She hoped to be surprised.

PART III

CHAPTER 29

CATE

July 2015, seven months later
New York City

The tubes pulling fluids in and out of her body angered Cate to the point of rage, but she couldn't tell anyone. Every now and then she built up the energy to scream at the top of her lungs, but it was just like the nightmare of her childhood: no matter how hard she screamed, no sound came out. She could not open her eyes or cry or shout inside the private room in New York-Presbyterian Hospital. She'd been in a coma after *Snowfall* capsized during heavy seas and wind off Rockaway Inlet and Coney Island three weeks ago. It was now seven months after Alex visited her in Provincetown. They had not spoken since and Cate had spent the time trying to put that part of her past behind her. Instead, she focused her energy on her painting and preparing to take her sailboat south to meet up with her parents.

Cate couldn't remember the details of what happened. All she remembered was fighting rough seas and incredibly challenging crosscurrents when her engine died. The winds pushed *Snowfall* to shore faster than it would have taken anyone to rescue her. Her rudder snapped against rocks and she lost the ability to steer. The vessel turned sideways as waves crashed against it. The last thing Cate remembered was hitting her head on the top of the companionway before everything went dark and cold.

She heard the words "persistent vegetative state" more than once. She heard her parents talking in hushed tones to doctors who sounded kind but who could not help her. She heard her mother cry for days, but then her mother stopped crying and started talking to her and playing music. Her parents took turns reading *Moby Dick* and *Anne of Green Gables* aloud. She loved hearing their voices. They almost lit up the darkness. Her mother must've brought in a portable CD player because Mozart and Adele and Spanish flamenco music played over and over again. Cate loved Adele's "Rolling in the Deep"—it almost made her feel as though she could open her eyes and go back to the land of the living. Sometimes she felt like she was snapping her fingers to the flamenco, swaying her hips to the hypnotic sound only to realize she was completely immobile and disconnected from her body. Her legs tingled like they were asleep when her mother rubbed lotion on her arms and legs and bent her joints back and forth, up and down, over and over again.

Cate knew she was in a coma. She knew she was partially asleep although her mind didn't need any sleep. She felt like she was in a heightened state of awareness for days and hours on end, thinking and wondering. She wondered if this is what it felt like to die when the soul passed on to another place, but the body was left behind. Sometimes she wondered if she was dead already. Her body was clearly no longer with her, and her mind seemed open to every particle of energy and knowledge all at once. Her dreams (or her thoughts, she couldn't tell the difference between the two) were vivid and sharp. She sailed aboard *Snowfall* on crystalline blue days as the wind filled the sails and the air was fragrant with salt and sun and warmth. She never felt hungry or thirsty or tired. She just was.

Suddenly she found herself sitting cross-legged in a circular room with people all around her. Everyone sang and rocked back and forth, and she somehow knew the words, but the language wasn't anything she recognized in all her travels throughout her life. Then the scene would change, and suddenly she'd be running in wide-open fields of grass, the buzzing sound of summer filling her ears. All of it was real. All of it was clear and beautiful and calm. All of it tantalized her senses, creating an overwhelming sense of contentment. She could travel anywhere in a flash and live in a new place at the mere thought of it. Greece. Spain. France. Canada. Every idea or thought was within reach of her imagination and her mind. She had never felt freer.

After Alex had left her in Provincetown, Cate spent Christmas alone, despite her parents' persistent urging for her to fly down to the Florida Keys to meet them for the holidays. As much as she loved her family, she couldn't do it. She couldn't spend the holidays with anyone. She just wanted to be alone. So, she spent the next eight months entirely on her own, with no lover, no family or friends in her immediate orbit. She spent the remainder of the winter in Provincetown painting and selling her art. As soon as the weather became warm enough, she moved out of her apartment and back aboard *Snowfall*. The warm spring allowed her to begin sailing south earlier than she expected. She planned to sail south to eventually meet up with her parents who were sailing north to meet her. She had not expected the storm in New York. She had not expected a lot of things.

Alex had been right that night in the Squealing Pig bar. At the time, she was so certain how things would have inevitably turned out between her and Alex, but one thing a coma teaches you is that life does not turn out quite the way you've expected. It also taught her that time was a gift that should not be squandered. And she had wasted so much time. Now she might not have any time left at all, but she had much she still wanted to say with no way to say it.

One day, as her mother played flamenco music and bent her knees back and forth, Cate imagined a steep and jagged ocean cliff like the ones she saw in Italy when she was a girl. Only, a golden, shimmering staircase was cut into the edge of the cliff. She climbed the stairs wearing something blue and flowing. She was barefoot. The wind was warm on her face and blew her long blond hair behind her. She felt the warm sun on her skin and heard seagulls *keow* and *ha-ha-ha* overhead. She climbed higher and higher, and the air became thinner. Finally, she reached the top of the staircase and saw a beautiful black wrought iron gate. Opening it, she walked through the gate, which creaked as she closed it behind her. Ahead of her was a beautifully manicured garden like Versailles on an even grander scale. There were so many paths to take, but she was drawn to a white gravel path to the left. She walked around a huge fountain of a mermaid spouting water, and as she passed it, the mermaid winked at her. She heard songbirds chirping and the rustle of the breeze through fruit trees, but her feet on the gravel made no sound at all. The air was fragrant with the smell of honeysuckle and lavender. She walked on until she saw a white tent next to a grove of cherry trees in full bloom. As she peeked inside, she could see candles lit. Something kept telling her to go in, so she pulled back the white canopy and entered the tent.

Her eyes took a long moment to adjust. It was dark inside the tent. The air was heavy with incense and burning candles. There was a couch in the middle of the tent with dark throw pillows. The tent was so inviting, Cate wanted to stay there forever. Suddenly, she saw someone sitting on the couch. She couldn't make out the figure so she took a few steps closer. The person rose to greet her. There, in the middle of the tent, was Alex. Her hair was brushed out straight and long and framed her face and her dark almond-shaped eyes. Alex smiled at her and Cate ran into her arms. Alex held her so tightly it was as she'd merely dreamed the boat and the cold water and the tubes in her arms, and this was the reality. Alex brushed Cate's curls away from her face and leaned forward and kissed her so deeply it was as if Cate had finally come home. The flamenco music played in the background and somewhere in the distance, Cate smelled the antiseptic smell of sickness and the hospital, but she pushed it aside, wanting to stay in this moment with Alex for as long as she could.

They sat on the couch and Alex took her hands in hers. They did not speak. Words were unnecessary. Everything that needed to be said was spoken through the conduit of energy that linked them together. The music filled the room and the incense swirled above her head. Every mistake she ever made in her life passed by her and drifted up into the air, disappearing. She had not lived her life well enough because she had not allowed herself to truly love and be loved. As Alex stared into her eyes in this place so real and so imaginary, Cate finally understood the sole meaning and purpose to her life, and she wanted so badly to get it right.

Cate knew she was close to death. She could feel it creeping into the edges of the room, blurring the walls into nothingness. She felt her breathing becoming shallower. She felt herself giving up. If only she could stay just another minute with Alex in this room, she would fight. She would fight for that.

CHAPTER 30

ALEX

July 2015
Positano, Italy

At the same time that Cate lay in a hospital bed in New York, Alex was half a world away. She heard a dog bark. Men spoke in Italian as they strolled past. Twilight snuck in like a fog, hiding the view of the jagged cliffs and whitewashed roofs below. Alex sat on the balcony of her private room atop the Hostel Brikette in Positano, Italy sipping a Coca-Cola as a warm breeze blew her long hair off her face. The single light of her travel candle illuminated the wrought iron table next to her. The air was swollen with the fragrant citrus smells of fresh lemon trees in full bloom.

Alex tried to capture it all in her travel journal. So far, she'd filled two notebooks on her trip through Italy. She'd been to Rome, Florence, Sorrento, and now Positano. Positano was by far her favorite. The vertical town was built along the cliffs with a backdrop of the gray pebble beaches and deep blue sea, each house a colorful shade of red, orange, or yellow. There was only one long and winding road in and one long and winding road out.

Exploring the town meant climbing and descending narrow, whitewashed stairs in every direction always leading to a half-hidden view that took your breath away. The town moved at its own pace compared to the cosmopolitan bustle of Rome or Florence.

After the narrow, winding roads were clear of tour buses (and the bus drivers stopped yelling at one another) and after the tourists had mostly disappeared into their hotels for the evening, the real town emerged. This was the time she liked best. The time after the day ended before the night began. It was her time to reflect and relax. It was her time to soak in all the experiences and sights of the day. Here she sat watching night float in, hiding the boats dotting the inlet, the colorful houses, and the sea below. Of all the places she had been, she felt as though she could live here, really live here in Positano, and be happy. The food, the people, the lemons, the colors, the ocean, all of it spoke to Alex's soul in a way nowhere else ever had.

She had been traveling so long and so far, that this was the first time she had the need to stop for a while and catch her breath. The idea of packing up and going somewhere else at this point exhausted her. But here in Positano, she could breathe. She could truly relax and write. She decided the next day to inquire about a longer-term rental and see if she could even get a temporary job at one of the hotels or tour companies. Her Italian wasn't great, but she was managing and every day in Italy helped that linguistic transition.

After the difficult meeting with Cate in Provincetown, she returned to Stockbridge for one week. In that time, she sold most of her furniture and put everything she wanted to keep—which wasn't much—into storage. Rather than selling her house, she decided to rent it. The income would pay her mortgage, taxes, and insurance and would give her a little extra every month. She still had the money from her father's death gratuity. Her mother had split the $100,000 evenly between her and Sara. She put hers away for a rainy day. This was the rainy day. She would use the $50,000 to travel around the world. She would go as far as the money would take her. Her sister and her mother thought she'd completely lost her mind. Hiking the Appalachian Trail was crazy to them, but this was downright insane. Alex didn't care. She had no reason to stay in Stockbridge any longer. The world was a vast, wondrous place that she would see with or without Cate by her side.

Cate. Not a day went by when she didn't think of her at least a dozen times. It might be the swirling colors of the setting sun over the horizon or a smiling little boy riding a bike for the first time. One day she saw an old woman tying a bundle of sticks outside her front door. The woman looked up at Alex, and her smile revealed several missing teeth. She looked as though she had lived a full life...as though she hadn't sat back and let life pass her by. Alex was taken with her and silently hoped one day she would look like that. There were moments every day Alex saved for Cate. She knew Cate would appreciate them the way she did and that had become enough for her.

Alex thought back to a night in Rome, when she uncharacteristically visited a gay bar that she read about online. Beige was an LGBTQ+ friendly restaurant, bar, and club in the hip Trastevere district located on the west bank of the Tiber south of Vatican City. By the time Alex arrived a little after ten o'clock, the club was crowded. She felt uncomfortable and a little out of place visiting a nightclub alone without speaking the language well. But she forced herself to go in and have at least one drink. She found a seat at the bar and ordered a cocktail. Two drinks later, she finally noticed an attractive blond woman smiling at her. She was definitely younger than Alex by about ten years. Alex felt the effects of the alcohol and decided to dance as Lady Gaga's music pulsed throughout the nightclub. She let go of her inhibitions, allowing the music to move her anyway it wanted to. The one thing about coming alone to a gay bar was that everyone on the dance floor was welcoming. Within minutes she felt like she was with a group of friends enjoying the night and the music.

Alex turned to see the blonde from the bar dancing next to her. They moved closer together, their bodies touching as the dance floor became more and more crowded. Alex was buzzed. The blond woman, to whom she had not even spoken a word, moved in for a sloppy, semidrunk kiss. Alex felt the woman's lips on hers, and it was all wrong. This woman didn't look like Cate or feel like Cate. She didn't smell like Cate, and she certainly didn't kiss like Cate.

Alex broke free and pushed her way out of the club leaving the woman alone on the dance floor. She couldn't get out of there fast enough. She quickly hopped into a cab and headed back to her hotel. Part of her had hoped she'd be able to meet someone and hook up. Lord knows she needed that. She needed to feel someone's skin against hers. She needed to feel the pleasure of someone else's hands upon her, but the sad fact remained that the only hands she wanted on her were Cate's. Anything else would be a poor, useless substitute. Alex learned her lesson that night: random hookups with strange women would never cure what ailed her. The idea of trying to meet someone for a serious relationship was out of the question. So, Alex did what she could. She continued to travel, write, and hope that someday things would be right between her and Cate.

Back in Positano, the candle burned out leaving her in almost total darkness and pulling her out of her own thoughts. She heard scooters zip by and the couple in the next room laughing. They were a sweet newlywed couple from Minnesota on their honeymoon. She'd shared a bottle of wine with them earlier but needed to get away and have her solitude. Being around a couple so happily in love wasn't easy for her. As she brushed her teeth, she heard her cell phone ring. She picked it up before even looking at the caller ID.

"Hello?" she said with a mouthful of toothpaste.

"Hello?" a strange female voice responded.

Alex rinsed her mouth out. "Hi. This is Alex. Who is this?"

"Oh, Alex. Thank God, it's you. This is Mrs. Conrad."

For the life of her, Alex couldn't figure out who this person was. "I'm sorry, do I know you?" Alex asked, completely confused.

"I'm Cate's mom. Cate Conrad?"

Cate's mother was calling her. Alex sat down on the bed.

"Hi, Mrs. Conrad. Is everything okay with Cate?"

There was a long pause on the other end of the line. Cate's mother said, "No, hon. Cate's not okay." Her voice broke, and Alex could hear her crying.

"Mrs. Conrad? What happened?"

"There's been an accident."

The floor fell out from underneath Alex. There couldn't be anything wrong with Cate. Not Cate. Cate was so strong, so sure, so confident. Nothing could ever touch her.

"What happened?" Alex asked.

"She was sailing down from the Cape to meet us. There was a sudden storm off the coast in New York. Cate capsized."

Alex could hear what Cate's mom was saying, but she was unable to process any of it. She heard a scooter as it passed outside. A dog barked four times. The couple next door laughed again. It was so peaceful in Positano. The night was so beautiful and full of life and possibility. It was so extraordinarily opposite what she was hearing on the other end of the line that she couldn't focus, she couldn't merge the place she was in with the words Cate's mother was speaking.

Mrs. Conrad continued. "Apparently her main engine failed, and she was unable to handle the currents or the waves. Her keel was snapped against rocks, and she somehow hit her head. I'm honestly not sure how she survived at all. A tugboat was able to reach her, and their crew pulled her out. Not only did they save Cate, but they also somehow managed to save the vessel. She's been in New York-Presbyterian Hospital for over two weeks now.

"Oh my God. Will she be okay? Can I talk to her?" Alex had so many questions, but all she wanted to do was hear Cate's voice to know she was okay.

"No, hon. That's why I'm calling you. She's in a coma. The doctors have called it a persistent vegetative state. They have no way of knowing how long it will last. She's breathing on her own, thank God, but she's got a feeding tube. She has a strict DNR and she told us more than once that if something like this ever happened she did not want to be kept like this forever. So, we're faced with an awful choice, but we thought you'd want to come see her before we made any decisions. I'm so sorry to dump all this on you, but there was no good way to tell you. I know you and my daughter were close. She has spoken of you more than once, and I know she would want you here. I'm sorry it's taken us so long to call you, but we didn't really know what was happening."

Alex sat on her bed, dumbfounded. She was in Italy enjoying life while Cate was in a coma fighting for hers. The mere thought of losing Cate forever made Alex more frightened than she'd ever been. Cate could not die. She could not leave her here alone for the rest of her life.

Alex tried to steady her voice to no avail. "Mrs. Conrad, thank you so much for calling me." Her voice wavered as she spoke. "I will get on a flight as soon as I can. I'm in Positano, Italy right now and it's about eleven o'clock at night. The closest airport is Naples, so I will get a flight out as soon as I'm able. Can you text me the details of the hospital?"

"Sure, Alex. I'll do that as soon as we hang up. Alex, if something should happen before you arrive, know that my daughter loved you very much."

The phone clicked dead. Alex felt shivers run up her spine and down her arms and legs. Cate's mother had said, "My daughter loved you very much." The words kept bouncing around the room. Sleep would be impossible tonight. She jumped up and immediately packed her bag, knowing she had to get on a plane as soon as possible. She called the emergency number listed in the room for the hostel and explained the situation. The owner offered to drive her himself to the Naples airport. Within an hour, Alex was on her way back to the States and back to Cate. She texted Sara, Marcie, and Emma to let them know what happened. All three of them offered to meet her in New York, but Alex said she wanted to do this alone, and she had no idea what she was walking into. She promised to keep them updated.

"Please, Cate. Wait for me. I'll be there soon," Alex whispered to the star-filled sky as the car sped through the deepening Italian night.

CHAPTER 31

CATE

July 2015
New York City

One moment Cate was aboard *Snowfall*, the next she sat at the same spot in the little Stockbridge restaurant Once Upon A Table. Everything looked exactly as it had the day she'd met Alex here and told her she did not love her. A waitress brought over a glass of water and handed her a menu. She looked at it although she wasn't hungry at all. She had no idea why she was even here.

A few moments later, the same waitress, a cute redhead who looked just out of college, returned to the table. "Hello," she said easily. "There is a letter." The waitress pulled an envelope from her apron pocket and handed it to Cate. It was in her handwriting with Alex's name written across the front.

Confused, Cate looked up at the waitress. "Wait, I'm not Alex. This letter can't be for me."

"I didn't say it was for you. It is by you." With that, the waitress left, and suddenly Cate found herself sitting somewhere peaceful in the mountains where a stream trickled by. Birds chirped and the sound of the breeze through the trees was intoxicating. Cate dipped her toes in the cold water and opened the envelope. It looked like her handwriting. She read it aloud.

Dear Alex:

I'm sitting by a stream in the middle of nowhere. As I watch the water flow downstream, constant and life-giving, I'm struck with the lesson that while so much has gone said and unsaid between us, it is all water under the bridge.

I've always made it my singular mission in life to live without regret because regret can swallow a person whole. Yet as I sit here contemplating the sum of my life thus far, the fact remains that I do regret some of my time with you. Not because of what transpired or didn't transpire but because I fell silent when I should not have. Those are the only moments in my life I wish I could have back to do over. The problem was, in those moments, I wanted to tell you so much. Even if you infuriated me by pushing too hard or wanting too much from me, from us, too fast, I could have said a great many things differently and therein lies my regret.

I have finally forgiven myself for falling in love with you. Lord knows I never meant to and I spent the better part of more than a few long months willing myself not to be in love. Even in this spectacularly peaceful place, your last words still ring out in my mind: "Coward. Manipulative bitch. Sick." I'm not sure I can or ever will forget how those words stung me and sting me now. If you were trying to wound me to my core the same way I had just hurt you, know that you succeeded.

The fact remains, I should never have made you feel anything but love. We've had so many signals crossed, you and I, that it's somehow hard to see through the vines and weeds sprouted by those crossed signals. But here in the woods, I finally see the truth. I should have only and ever made you feel love. Nothing else will ever matter as much as that. Clearly, I've failed in that regard, and for that, I am so sorry.

Life is a magical gift that never turns out the way we expect it to. But of all the roads I've traveled, of all the bridges I've burned, all of it has brought me here to this place both literally and figuratively. I am here because I was meant to be. But no matter where I go or where you are, we are both connected from a soul place, deep and true. You are my twin soul, Alex. We are half of the same whole, opposites reflecting back the best, and the worst in each other, and ourselves. I fall asleep at night dreaming you are next to me, and in those dreaming moments I bask in the glow of our love because somewhere, in some other dimension, in some lifetime beyond here, we are lovers and best friends and twin flames reunited. Everything that has happened will happen, and is happening right now. I see that finally for the first time.

I love you whether I see your face again or whether you ever forgive me or love me back. All of my words, letters, and paintings are pieces of this love, angles of the same mirror reflecting back. I give myself permission to love you, and I give myself permission to love myself for loving you so completely. No matter how many years go by, I take you with me.

Yours always,
Cate

Just as Cate finished reading the letter, the paper transformed into dozens of purple and yellow butterflies that flew from her hands out into the trees and the sky. She felt such relief and so much love she laid her head down against the cool moss and fell asleep.

CHAPTER 32

ALEX

July 2015
New York City

Alex stared at the red lights of the elevator flashing as it moved up from the main lobby to the Department of Neurology & Neurosurgery. Once the doors opened, she raced out to the first nurse's station and asked where the Neurological ICU was located. She was directed to the left down a long, white fluorescent-lit hallway. She barely mumbled her thanks before running down the hall, her black Converse sneakers squeaking against the shiny floors.

She stopped at two more nurses' stations before finally making her way to the right room. The door was closed. Alex peeked in, holding her breath. She was not prepared for the sight of Cate lying in a white hospital bed looking nearly dead but not quite. Tears sprang from her eyes, but she angrily wiped them away. She would not cry right now. Cate would hate that.

The door opened and a woman who looked so much like Cate but a little shorter with dark eyes, came toward her, as well as an older man with Cate's bright blue eyes.

"You must be Alex," said the woman in a voice so much like Cate's, it shook Alex to the core. All she could do was nod yes.

Cate's mother took her elbow and sat her down in a chair outside the room. "Let's talk here for a moment," she said kindly. Cate's father sat on the other side of her. Alex knew she must look insane. She hadn't showered or eaten in over a day, having come straight from Naples as fast as she could. Cate's father must have been psychic because he said, "Don't worry, you look fine. You're just beautiful. Drink some water. I'm sure you came straight from the airport."

Again, Alex nodded and blinked. It was as if her ability to speak had left her. She gratefully accepted the water and drank half the bottle. She felt her cells expand as the liquid passed through her body.

"Thank you," she said shakily. "I'm sorry." She was amazed Cate's parents were so kind and concerned for her while their daughter lay in a coma in the next room. Cate's father had the kindest eyes she had ever seen, and her mother's hair, well it was no surprise where Cate got her long blond curly hair.

"Before we go in, there are a few things you should know," Cate's father said calmly. "We don't know if she has any brain damage. We don't know if she can hear us or is aware of us at all, but I'd like to think she is right here with us. Her vital functions are stable right now. She is breathing on her own. We've been in a holding pattern to see if she will just wake up. We are trying to keep our conversations with her positive, happy, and peaceful."

Alex nodded. She wanted so much to be at Cate's side, but she was terrified of what she would see.

"Are you sure you're ready?" Cate's mother asked.

"Yes. I'm ready." Alex mustered every ounce of strength she possessed.

"Then go ahead, dear.

Alex hesitated a long moment before pulling the door open and walking in.

~

CATE

Cate felt like she was flying. The sky above was a light blue with wispy clouds that looked like cotton candy pulled too thin. The next moment she walked on a pink sand beach that could have been the Bahamas or Bermuda. No matter where she went in her life, the beach was always her real home. She could stand in the same place at the water's edge for a full day and night and watch the view change every second. She felt calm and at peace, although she still heard the annoying beeping and humming of electronics somewhere in the background. That bothered her. She tried to pretend they weren't there so she dipped her toes into the water. It was so warm. She smelled the salt in the air and wondered what month it was. Maybe July or September. It didn't matter. The breeze was light against her face and the sky changed colors every second as if she was somehow watching the aurora borealis. Every cell in her body felt comfortable and easy, weightless and carefree. She wished she could tell Alex all about this place. She wished they could take a long walk hand in hand together on this wide expanse of beach and just talk. Just then, she heard something so far away, it was barely audible. She tried to silence the waves rolling into shore to make out the sound but she couldn't quite capture it. She strained to hear it.

"Cate. Cate. Cate" echoed far off in the distance. The voice. Someone was saying her name. Who was it? The voice was familiar, and unusually comforting.

"Cate. I'm here. Come back to me please."

Cate smiled. She knew that voice. It was Alex. Was Alex here on this beach with her? She looked around but saw no one, the voice was there with her somehow, floating in the air above the seagulls and the ocean surf. She wanted so badly to go swimming and dip her head beneath the waves. She took a few steps, letting the warm and soothing salt water cover her ankles, then her calves, and her knees. Still, the voice called out to her.

"I'm here," Cate said aloud, smiling to the empty beach. The water pulled her deeper and so she took a few more steps until the water covered her waist and her belly button. She wanted to dive in and swim fast and free, but she didn't. She was waiting for something, for someone. She dipped her hand into the warm water and pulled it out, fascinated by the droplets of water in perfect luminescent domes as they slid down her hand into the water. She heard her name far off in the distance as if it were a promise of something wonderful to come.

ALEX

Alex stood at Cate's bedside. She held her hand. All of Cate's color was gone, and she was as white as the sheets that were wrapped around her slim body. Cate's blond curly hair even looked bland and dull, all of its life sucked away by the tubes coming out of her hand. Alex had promised she would not cry but she could not stop the onslaught of tears that fell from her face onto Cate's fingers. She squeezed Cate's hand.

"Please, Cate. Wake up. I have so much to tell you. We have a life to live together. We have memories to make together. I'll go anywhere with you. If you want to live on a boat, we can live on a boat. If you want to live in a shoe, I'll live in a shoe. I don't care where we live or where we go so long as I'm with you. You are my home. Oh, Cate. Wake up. I love you. I need you. You can't leave me here alone. I'll never love anyone the way I love you. If you don't wake up I'll end up being mad at you forever. Is that what you want?

CATE

Cate turned in the direction of the sun as it set low and orange on the horizon. She felt as though she was taking one last long look at it because she would never see a sunset like that again. That made her sad, but the voice that called to her from deep inside the waves was a strong and urgent pull. She took another step as the water covered her chest and neck. She no longer felt the sand between her toes because she was somehow weightless and floating even though she knew she wasn't. She felt like she had nothing else to do but dip her head in the water. As if that was the sum total of what she always ever had to do her whole life. And so, she did. She held her breath and went under.

ALEX

Alex bent forward and kissed Cate's cool, dry lips. She brushed away a stray strand of hair like she always did. She held Cate's hand tightly, and let the fingers of her other hand trace Cate's jawline and the edge of her chin. She let her hand fall to that place she loved to kiss just beneath Cate's ear. She wanted to climb into bed and curl up next to Cate, but Cate looked so frail and small Alex was afraid she would break her. If she could trade places with her, she'd do it in a second. Cate was meant to be alive and smiling, sailing, and catching the sun on her face, painting with vibrant colors. Cate was not meant to be here in this sunless, darkened room with fluorescent lights and tubes and machines that beeped and clicked and grew on her like ivy on a rock wall. They had been so foolish wasting time being stubborn and selfish. Now they had no time left and all Alex wanted to do was rewind the clock and go back to the first time she saw Cate in school so she could start all over again, and do things a little differently.

Just as Alex was about to let go of Cate's hand she stopped. She looked again at Cate's closed eyes. Something felt different. The air had shifted in the room. Alex felt a light breeze and swore she could smell the ocean. It was an odd sensation. Alex knew better. She was perfectly awake and aware, and she wasn't so exhausted that she was hallucinating. But still, she felt it. She turned her head and looked out the window in the direction of the sun setting across the cold metallic New York skyline. She sighed and closed her eyes. And then she felt it. Cate's fingers tightened around hers.

Alex's eyes shot from the sunset out the window to Cate's face. As if she was awake all along, Cate looked back at her with wide, blue eyes that Alex realized had become several shades darker. Alex leaned in toward Cate's face to make sure she didn't imagine it and Cate whispered clear as day, "What took you so long?"

CHAPTER 33

CATE

A week after Cate woke from her coma, she was released from the hospital under strict instructions to rest and avoid too much outside stimulation. She felt fine except for the weakness and exhaustion. It was as if her body lost all of its muscle and endurance, and it frustrated her to no end. Alex was with her each day, helping her do exercises, forcing her to eat and drink, reading to her, and telling her awful jokes. One day she even brought in a book of Mad Libs to help pass the time. Cate's mom and dad were also there every day. It seemed to Cate that her mother and father genuinely liked Alex and enjoyed her company. In fact, they had been ganging up on her of late to take it easy, which annoyed Cate too. Whenever she woke from a nap or struggled to do something basic like bend over and tie a shoe, Alex was there to make her smile, to guide her, and to cheer her on.

They had not talked at all about Cate's experiences while she was in the coma. She remembered all of it in vivid detail but didn't feel ready to talk about it, as if talking about it would somehow make it less real or less a part of her. She still didn't remember much of anything about the night of the accident aboard *Snowfall* and the doctors said those memories may or may not come back to her at all. The events of that night weren't that important to her. The events after that night, which brought Alex back to her, were all that mattered.

She had so much she wanted to say to Alex but the time wasn't right. She wanted to focus 100 percent on recuperating enough to be discharged from the hospital. Her life had taken a drastic, nearly incomprehensible turn and she was still reeling from the place she now found herself. It was as if she was still in a sort of dream. The idea that she would capsize and nearly drown aboard a boat was as foreign to her as sitting atop the Great Wall of China and eating a turkey sandwich. She just couldn't wrap her brain around the idea that the one place she had always felt the safest had been the most treacherous of all. For now, she was happy to be on dry land and to have the people who mattered most to her so close.

Cate had two specific requests immediately upon her release from the hospital. First, she wanted to go to Central Park, where she took off her shoes to walk barefoot in the grass. She needed to feel the cool, damp earth under her feet. She'd spent so much time in the coma floating and flying around that the sensation of being firmly planted on the ground soothed her in a way nothing else had so far. She closed her eyes and walked around as if she was trying to settle herself back down to earth for the remainder of her life.

The extremely hot July weather sapped all of Cate's remaining energy, and she dozed off in the taxi cab, her head tucked against Alex's shoulder until they reached stop number two, the Atlantis Marina on Staten Island. Apparently, the towboat captain's brother owned the marina, which had boat repair capabilities. Alex held Cate's arm as they walked down the dock to *Snowfall*, which looked pretty bad next to all the other pristine sailboats on the dock. *Snowfall*'s mast was broken in two, the rigging and mainsail hanging limply like a broken arm. The hull was scratched up badly, but it was floating and had survived the ordeal just as Cate had. They carefully boarded the vessel. The marina owner had been kind enough to clean up the interior and drain it of water. It smelled musty, but it would be livable again after considerable work and cleaning, neither of which Cate was up to at this moment. She just ran her hands down the sides of the boat and silently thanked it for keeping her alive. She believed the boat was special the night she named it, and now there was no doubt.

She didn't stay aboard long. Something about feeling the boat shift under her feet unsettled her, but she wanted to see the boat and thank it. They would both have scars from their ordeal forever, but they both had made it through alive. Cate was suddenly exhausted. She wanted to go home to rest but she had no idea where that would be.

After much deliberation, her parents decided to fly down to Virginia Beach to get their sailboat out of the water and have it driven back up to New York where they would dock it and live aboard for as long as it took Cate to recover completely. They'd be gone for about a week. In the meantime, Alex would take Cate to Brooklyn to recuperate. Her friend Marcie serendipitously had a work colleague who owned a house in Green Point, Brooklyn. She was away traveling the world with her new rich boyfriend, and so Alex had a place to stay for as long as she wanted or needed, as long as she watered the plants.

Cate's mother hugged her tightly as if she didn't want to ever let her go. "Mom, please, you're strangling me. It's okay. I'm all right."

"I know, honey. I know. It's just, I love you so much," her mother gushed, wiping tears from her eyes. Cate's father hugged her tighter than he ever had before. All at once, he seemed older. The last month had aged him considerably. He was too choked up to speak and simply held his daughter close and told her without words how much he loved her.

Cate was beyond surprised when her parents hugged Alex

with as much force and emotion as they had shown when embracing her. "Thank you, Alex," was all her mother said, but in that thank-you was a world of relief and understanding that Alex's love for Cate had brought her back from near death.

"Don't worry, Mrs. Conrad. I'll take good care of her," said Alex firmly.

"I know you will, honey. Call if you need anything. We'll see you soon."

Cate watched her parents hop into the waiting taxi, and Alex's hand found hers and squeezed it.

"Now what?" Cate asked.

"Let's go home," Alex said simply.

$\sim$

Alex

Alex was nervous as she took Cate back to the house in Brooklyn. It wasn't as if this was her home, but she had been living here for a week since flying back from Naples. It wasn't the place she was worried about; it was how she and Cate would get along now that the trauma and hospital stay had ended. They hadn't talked about anything of substance since that conversation in Provincetown so many months before, but none of it mattered. Time had stretched out like a ribbon across their separate lives and had almost been cut short. This time she wouldn't get ahead of herself. She promised to just remain in the moment with Cate, whatever that moment was. She would not push to make things any more or any less than exactly what they were because all she had asked was for Cate to be with her, and she was. Her prayer had been answered and for that Alex would always be incredibly grateful.

Still, she was tense. She wasn't sure if they would pick back up the way they were before or if things would be awkward. She wanted Cate to be comfortable, and no one was sure if there were any long-term side effects from the trauma. Only time would tell. Alex tried to be nonchalant about welcoming Cate inside. The building was an old ambulance depot, so the layout was a little strange and all on one floor, but it was clean and bright and comfortable with the added blessing of central air conditioning.

After she showed Cate around, Alex noticed Cate looked worn out and tired so she suggested they take a nap. She was going to make something to eat, but the way Cate was wobbling back and forth, Alex opted for the nap first. Without speaking, Alex led Cate to the bedroom and drew the shades to block out the bright summer sun. Cate climbed onto the queen-sized bed and lay down atop the covers. Alex turned to leave.

"No, stay with me, please," Cate said.

Alex lay down next to Cate. For a few moments, they lay on their backs side by side, not touching. Alex closed her eyes and sighed. She was more tired than she realized. The past couple of weeks had taken all of her reserves. She hadn't realized she'd been operating in a constant state of high alert with Cate and how little attention she had paid to herself. She was worn out. It was as if she could finally let down her guard and relax. The waves of exhaustion washed over her and she dozed off almost immediately.

In the moments before she fell asleep, Cate turned onto her side and the mattress creaked slightly. Alex felt Cate's arm come across her chest. She initially thought she was imagining it as she had done so many times before over the last months. But no, this was real. Alex realized Cate was trying to hold her. She turned on her side so she and Cate could spoon. Cate shifted her body and snuggled tightly against Alex. Alex felt Cate's steady, warm breath against her neck and within seconds, the two were fast asleep.

CHAPTER 34

CATE

Cate woke to the smell of something heavenly cooking. She had been craving a cup of coffee but had not been allowed any in the hospital. She reached over in bed to make sure Alex wasn't still next to her, which of course she wasn't. She was cooking. Cate rose and looked at herself in the full-length mirror. She looked undeniably awful. She'd lost at least ten pounds in the hospital, and her hair was a tangled mess. The sudden urge to shower overtook her hunger pains.

Thirty minutes later, Cate felt and looked much better. She borrowed a pair of Alex's shorts and a tank top from her suitcase on the floor and padded down the hall to the kitchen where Alex had prepared a spread fit for a queen. Cate scanned a table overflowing with freshly squeezed orange juice, French press coffee (decaffeinated to be safe), plus scrambled eggs, hash brown potatoes, bacon, and fruit salad. Alex had even placed a single red rose in a vase on the kitchen table. Cate's first thought was that this could become a regular weekend tradition for them, enjoying a big breakfast together and allowing the day to unfold however it may. The look on Alex's face as she held a spatula up and waved was all so domestic and sweet it took Cate's breath away. This was the life she had been afraid of. This was what she had been fighting against all that time, and at that exact moment, it was all so utterly ridiculous she laughed.

"What's so funny?" Alex asked, a hint of hurt rising in her voice.

"Nothing. This is wonderful. You're wonderful," said Cate, still taking in the entire scene as if she was memorizing it. She knew she would remember this moment many years later when they were old. This was the moment she would always return to because it was the moment she finally understood that all she ever wanted was someone to love, someone to call home—and she had her, egg-laden spatula and all.

Cate walked toward Alex and gently pulled the spatula from her hand, laying it on the table. The expression on Alex's face was one of surprise, and yes, vulnerability. Cate saw Alex standing before her with no guard up. She was open and honest, true and so trusting. It made Cate's heart beat a little harder, and she felt such tenderness for Alex she could no longer contain it. She simply took Alex's hands in hers and said, "I love you," and kissed her ever so gently on the lips.

~

ALEX

At first, Alex wasn't sure if she heard it right. Cate said I love you, the three words she had hoped to hear for so long. Alex's entire body and soul relaxed into Cate's kiss. It wasn't a tear-your-clothes-off kiss. She was hoping that would come later. It was a you-are-the-love-of-my-life kind of kiss. It was a kiss that showed everything they'd been thinking passed between them without words, without explanation, and without judgment. They both had to learn how to stand completely on their own two feet before they could stand together and they had done that. This kiss was filled with mutual respect and tenderness, and above all, hope. Alex felt the butterflies in her stomach bounce around and just like that her stomach growled, loud. It broke the spell between them and Cate pulled away. When Alex opened her eyes, she saw Cate's eyes staring back at her, twinkling with amusement.

"I think we'd better eat this amazing breakfast you cooked." Cate smiled.

They sat and began to devour the food. Alex saw the way Cate's eyes closed in pure satisfaction when she took her first sip of the hot coffee.

"Oh my God. This coffee. I have been craving coffee something fierce," Cate said in between a mouthful of scrambled eggs.

After they polished off the eggs and bacon, Cate picked at the remaining hash browns.

"That hit the spot," she said patting her belly.

Alex smiled.

"What's wrong? You've been awfully quiet," Cate asked gently.

Alex took a moment to respond. She was still so overwhelmed. She and Cate were together. Cate was safe. Cate had said I love you. It was almost more than she could handle all at once and she found herself tongue-tied in a way that was truly unusual for her.

"I know, it's a lot to take in," Cate said, reading Alex's mind. "And did I get this right that you were in Italy before you came here to be with me?"

"Yeah. I was in Positano staying at this incredible little hostel. I'd been traveling around Italy for about a month actually. I've been writing a lot and I'm hoping to turn my experiences into a book, but I'm not quite sure what that will look like yet."

"Alex, that's amazing. I feel like you've become this entirely different person with all the hiking and traveling."

"I'm still the same person I was before," Alex replied, shrugging her shoulders.

"You are in all the ways that matter. I just think it's incredible that you've done so much with your life these past months."

"I wanted to understand what you loved so much about living that way."

"Oh, I don't know. I think there is something just as valuable about having a home and someone who loves you by your side no matter where you are," said Cate.

"You did say 'I love you,' didn't you?" asked Alex suddenly, her eyes wide. "I heard that right?"

Cate laughed. "Yes. You heard that right. I love you. I'm sorry it took me so long to figure that out. Well, that's not what I mean." Cate stopped and paused for a moment. "Here's the thing. I loved you right away, I think. When you told me you loved me, I felt the same way. I was just too afraid to admit it to myself, let alone say it aloud to you. I never told you this, but when I was sixteen years old, we stayed for a while in the Bahamas and I fell in love with a girl named Amelia. It was the first time I fell in love, and I was head over heels in love with her. Obviously, we were just sixteen so the idea of it being any more than a summer fling was ridiculous, but I was clueless and young. On my last day before we sailed out, I told her I loved her, and she basically ignored me. That night I saw her making out with some guy. It broke my heart, and I promised myself I'd never get close enough to anyone to run the risk of it happening again.

"Then you came along, and everything changed. I fell in love with you much more deeply than I ever knew was possible at sixteen years old. It terrified me." Cate's voice was steady, sure, and calm. "Alex, I'm not proud of what I did to you, and I'd like to spend the rest of my life making it up to you if you'll let me." She looked intently at Alex.

Alex almost couldn't believe her ears. Everything she had hoped to understand about Cate was there, shared between them honestly. "Why didn't you tell me any of this before?" Alex asked, her voice filled with emotion.

"I'm not sure, partly because I wasn't able to articulate it to myself. It's a hard lesson to learn, but I've learned a lot of things about myself since you walked into my life," Cate answered matter-of-factly.

Alex rose from her chair and walked toward Cate. The physical distance between them at the kitchen table was too much. She needed to touch her, to feel her body. Her self-restraint went right out the window. She took Cate's hand and pulled her up. Without a word, she led her to the bedroom. Facing Cate, she brushed a stray curl away from her forehead and placed both hands on either side of her face, kissing her deeply. The slow burn pilot light inside Alex exploded into a full-on flame at the precise moment she felt the tip of Cate's tongue touch hers. Their kiss deepened. The space between their bodies was erased completely. Cate pulled off Alex's tank top as well as her own. In a matter of moments, they were both naked and touching. Alex felt the softness of Cate's skin on hers. She pulled Cate down on the bed on top of her. She needed to feel every inch of Cate's body. Close was not close enough. Every fiber of Alex's being yearned to connect with Cate. They touched each other like it was the first time all over again. This time, they knew that being together was a gift almost stolen from them far too soon.

"Are you okay? Should we stop?" asked Alex, breaking lip contact, concerned this was all too much too fast for Cate.

"Stop talking," Cate said, her breathing heavy. "I'm fine. I'm more than fine." She covered Alex's mouth with hers.

Alex wanted to go slowly. She wanted to be gentle and loving, but the ache to be inside of Cate overwhelmed her. Cate besieged her senses completely: her smell, her touch, and her body, all of it. Alex's lips moved down Cate's neck and hovered at the spot where she could feel her pulse. She could almost hear Cate's pounding heartbeat in her own head. As her lips glided down Cate's neck to her breasts, Cate's body rose up to meet her, urging her to touch every inch of her. Alex's tongue played with Cate's hardened nipples, causing her to moan in pleasure. She could feel the muscles in her own pelvis expand and contract. Her tongue and lips began to glide down Cate's belly.

Suddenly, Cate rolled Alex over, so she was on top. "No, I need to taste you now." She pinned Alex's arms gently over her own head as she kissed her deeply.

"Cate please," Alex whispered.

Cate's mouth and tongue drifted down Alex's body, quickly lingering for a long moment over her hips. Unable to wait any longer, Alex grabbed the back of the headboard with both hands and pushed her hips up against Cate's mouth. Within seconds, Cate's tongue found its mark.

Alex drew in a huge breath and held it. Time stopped. Flecks of dust hovered in the air above them, suspended. All of the wishing and all of the wanting, all of the steps walked on a jagged trail and moonlit nights on the open water led them both here to this place, this singular moment in time. Cate's tongue undulated and caressed, licked and commanded Alex's body to respond to her and only her.

Alex tried hard not to orgasm too quickly. She willed herself to wait because she never wanted Cate to stop what she was doing. She felt wave after wave building and falling back within her and Cate's tongue matched those sensations completely. Alex moaned but held herself back, eyes squeezed shut.

"Alex, let it go," Cate commanded.

Alex felt the last remaining wall between them crumble. Cate's tongue dipped over and over again deep inside her, the crests rising within Alex as her body met Cate's mouth. The waves continued building, one after the other, and she swore she smelled the ocean. She knew this was the place she would cling to until every ounce of breath left her body. There was no separation between them. No doubt or uncertainty...only this merging, this complete and utter intoxicatingly beautiful sensory-overload connection. They were finally plugged into each other in a way that lifted them both to a higher plane, a higher level that defied gravity or time or space or anything made of this world.

Alex exploded with such force that she left all thought behind. The orgasm that rocked her entire being burst forth from somewhere so deep within her she felt her body leave her, and her soul rise up and fly. The first shockwave wasn't even the biggest. Again, and again, the orgasms rolled through her body, one smaller followed by a second that caused her to cry out in a voice she did not recognize as her own.

Cate's lips moved back up Alex's body. She kissed Alex deeply again as Alex wrapped her arms around her back, pulling at her blond mane of hair. "I'll never stop loving you," Cate whispered in her ear as her tongue flicked Alex's earlobe.

Without warning, Cate dove her fingers deep inside Alex as Alex tried desperately not to dig her fingernails into Cate's smooth and strong back. She pulled at Cate's long hair with one hand and had to feel her with the other. Within seconds, she pushed Cate's legs apart and drew her fingers deep inside Cate's swollen, throbbing folds. The two matched a rhythm, rocking and pulling and pushing again and again until the edges of their bodies blended together until there was nothing that separated one from the other. Alex felt Cate's body tighten around her fingers. She felt the rush of warmth and wetness as Cate came against her and as her own body released itself completely for Cate.

Sweat covered their bodies as they slid back and forth over the other, under the other, drawing moans and cries and breath from each other until there was nothing left. Gone were the doubt and uncertainty. There was only this. Nothing else mattered. Nothing else would ever matter more.

Cate trailed her fingertips down Alex's back and caressed the small of her back. Alex was exhausted but didn't want Cate to stop touching her like this.

"I heard your voice when I was in the coma," Cate said, her

voice barely above a whisper.

Alex rolled onto her side and gazed at Cate, mesmerized by those bright blue eyes. "You did?"

"I heard everything: the music playing, my parents reading to me, all of it. It was like I could float in and out of the room. Even when my mind was somewhere else, I could hear what was happening in the room. All of it was so vivid and clear. There's something important I need to tell you," Cate began earnestly as her fingers continued to caress Alex's back.

"Okay," said Alex, tenderly running her finger down Cate's jawline.

"Right before I woke up, I was on a beach that looked a lot like the Bahamas or maybe Bermuda. The sand was pink. It was sunset, and the sky was this amazing color that I would never be able to describe with words. It was out-of-this-world beautiful but familiar at the same time. Even in the middle of all that beauty, I heard the beeping of the machines in the background, and I could even smell the antiseptic hospital room. Anyway, I kept being drawn into the water so I started stepping into it, a little at a time. The water was so warm and comfortable. I knew I was dying. I knew that was the moment that I'd leave my body forever and I was okay and fine with it. I was ready. Then I heard your voice calling to me. I heard everything you said. It was weird. It was like the same water I was walking into to end my life was the same water I needed to submerge in to begin it again. So, I kept walking in, deeper and deeper, staring at the sunset until I went underwater completely."

"And then what happened? Alex asked, her eyes still fixed intently on Cate's.

"Then I woke up and squeezed your hand and it was like I was there all along just waiting for you to come and find me."

Alex wrapped Cate tightly in her arms. "I'm here," she whispered as she lightly kissed Cate's forehead and cheeks, eyelids, and lips. "I'll always be right here." Something occurred to Alex. She leaned up on an elbow. "Right before you woke up I looked out the window at the hospital. The light from the sun broke through the clouds, and I turned to look at it. The sunset was unbelievable. I bet it was the same sunset we saw."

"Maybe," said Cate. And after a pause, "Alex I know that in Provincetown I told you I couldn't imagine our life together because we both wanted different things."

"Look, let's not put pressure on things. You just got out of the hospital. Let's take it slow and see where things lead. I'm in no rush for anything to be except what it is right now."

Cate sat up and pulled Alex up with her so the two faced each other. "Well, that's the thing. I am in a rush. I know what's important now and I don't want to waste another second. I never want you to feel doubt again." She drew Alex's legs over hers and pulled her even closer. "I never want you to feel like we're not on the same page. I want to be with you. If that means living in Stockbridge or Kansas, I don't care. All that's important to me is that we are together and that you know every day how much I love you. And I'd really like it if you could give me that journal one more time. This time I'll savor it." She smiled and kissed Alex gently.

"I don't have it," answered Alex truthfully. "After that awful day, I tore all the pages apart piece by piece and threw it in the trash. It's long gone."

"Oh, babe. I'm so sorry." Cate held her close and kissed her forehead. "Please forgive me."

"I forgave you a long time ago. I don't have that journal to give back to you, but I did write you a bunch of letters in my journal as I hiked the Appalachian Trail. I never sent them to you because, well, I was afraid to," Alex said.

"I would very much like to read them. All of them."

"Even though you already know how I feel?" Alex pushed Cate back down on the bed and began kissing her neck and earlobes.

"Just in case I missed something important." Cate's voice seemed to catch as Alex drew her tongue down her body again.

CHAPTER 35

July 2016
The Florida Keys

The setting sun reflected over the clear aquamarine water after a picture-perfect summer day in the Florida Keys. The only sound Alex could hear was the rushing of the wind through the rigging and the waves in their steady drumbeat against the hull. She shielded her eyes with one hand and looked over at Cate who was in full control of a repaired and gleaming *Snowfall* from the cockpit. Wearing a faded blue oxford shirt and a pair of khaki shorts, Cate leaned against the large steering wheel with her golden tanned left leg propped up on the seat of the cockpit. Her hair flew out behind her in a long, curly, shimmering wave that snapped in the wind. It had been a year since her accident, and they had only been apart a few days in all that time.

After staying in Brooklyn for a few blissful weeks to begin repairs on *Snowfall*, they'd returned to Stockbridge for the winter, moving into Sara and David's finished basement since Alex's house was rented. At first, Alex thought it would be difficult to return to Stockbridge without actually living in her beloved home, she soon realized that her house was just a place but her home was with Cate, no matter where it was.

Cate spent a great deal of time with Alex's family, and Sara and David welcomed her as if she had always been there. Oddly enough, Alex's mom hit it off with Cate. So much so that after dinner one night, she pulled her daughter aside and said, "I'm so happy you found someone like Cate. Your father would have liked her very much." Her mother had never been able to talk about Alex's sexuality before, so that was a huge step, one Alex appreciated greatly.

They spent the winter planning what they wanted to do. It was important for Cate to get back to sailing to overcome her fear of capsizing again and they decided to spend one year on the water.

Alex tipped her head back and looked up at the sky. Her eyes could barely capture the pure vastness of the sea and sky merged together in the thin line of the horizon. She wondered if this is what her father used to feel when he flew jet planes at Mach speed across the sky. Although they never discussed it, she bet her father also needed to capture the instant the sun slipped below the horizon. She felt him there now, high above her, looking down and smiling. She turned her head in the direction of the sun and felt the last remaining warmth hit her face. She closed her eyes.

There are moments in life that take our breath away and moments that define the rest of our days. These moments fill our minds with memories that have such clarity, we can recall exact details dozens of years later as if they had only just occurred. The extraordinary moment when Alex met Cate was that crossroads, that moment in time when the course of both their lives was altered forever. For that, Alex would always be grateful.

Time could pass however it was meant to, slow, fast, with considerable difficulty, or in a fleeting instant of perfection or pain. It would be what it would be. It was no longer about becoming someone or finding someone or needing someone to come back. It was no longer about walking mile after mile to find out what she was made of or to push her own boundaries until they burst. It was about being who she was in that moment with someone who loved her. The heart will always want what the heart wants. Sometimes it makes a choice that the mind cannot comprehend. It's said that the heart of a woman is one of the great mysteries of the universe, but Alex's heart was no longer a mystery to her. Neither was Cate's. They both had depths she never knew existed, but now she knew exploring those depths with Cate was all that mattered.

They had come so far. The ocean stretched out before them with infinite possibility, grace, love, and hope. Alex's heart was full. She was grateful for all of it. *Only Love.* She thought back to the carving in a shelter on the Appalachian Trail. Now, she understood those words. Now, she embraced them. She looked over at Cate, who smiled back at her as if she knew exactly what she was thinking. Alex McKenzie was finally the person she thought she was, and it was enough.

THE END.

ACKNOWLEDGMENTS

Part of *In the Direction of the Sun* was written during several section hikes of the Appalachian Trail in multiple states. I am grateful to the Appalachian Trail Conservancy, the Potomac Appalachian Mountain Club, Shenandoah Park Ranger Patressa Kearns, and everyone at the Rapidan Mountain Retreat including Mike Robison and all the fine fly-fishing gentlemen from cabin three who welcomed me, fed me steak, and told me some fantastic stories. Thank you to all the hikers I've met along the Trail and to Billy Goat for hiking with me here and there.

I'm indebted to Judy Long for her patient answers to my fumbling questions on sailing and navigation, as well as to the Women Who Sail Group for their input and information about circumnavigation, sailboats, and sailing life in general.

Sincere thanks to Dallas Greene of City and Colour (www.cityandcolour.com) and Tricia Ricciuto of Bedlam Music Management for your generosity and assistance. Dallas, your lyrics and your music rock.

Thank you to my supportive and talented editor, Nikki Busch for working so hard to bring out the best in me and in this manuscript.

Finally, thank you to all my generous readers and fans. I.V. now and always.

ABOUT THE AUTHOR

Lucy J. Madison is an author of fiction, non-fiction, and poetry, and is a credited screenwriter from Connecticut. She's solo-hiked over 800 miles of the Appalachian Trail (and counting). She enjoys writing stories for women, and about women. Lucy is currently hard at work on her third novel. She received a Master of Arts in Liberal Studies from Wesleyan University and resides with her wife of nearly 20 years in shoreline Connecticut and Province-town, Massachusetts along with their beloved pets.

She loves receiving emails and notes from readers!

Contact Lucy!
www.lucyjmadison.com
info@lucyjmadison.com

MORE FROM LUCY J. MADISON

Personal Foul

Named one of the Top 10 Lesbian Sports Romances by
The Romance Review.

"The ending was grand and the sex scenes were so hot and so well written...LOVED IT. WOW."

"This is a great read...I highly recommend reading this book to see that love is possible no matter which side of the line you're on." – *The Lesbian Review*

"The main characters' make up was sexy and steamy...utterly romantic and perfect. 5 Stars"

– Inked Rainbow Reads

Kat Schaefer's career is on autopilot. She's an elite basketball official in the WNBA after surviving an extremely rocky childhood but still finds herself adrift in her personal life almost two years after her longtime girlfriend dumped her. Kat's well-ordered world turns upside down again when she meets a hotshot rookie named Julie Stevens who knocks her world off balance with her stellar play and captivating eyes.

Despite Kat's best defense, she falls hard for the young player but she's unable to open herself up to love again. Her solution is to retreat alone to the magnificent beaches of Provincetown, Massachusetts to heal old wounds and to figure out what the future holds for both of them.